# INTERVENTION

I0565026

# HEIDI HARRIS

*Heidi Harris*

*First Publication 2015*

*This book is completely fictional.*

*Any resemblance to anyone is purely coincidental.*

*All rights belong to Heidi Harris.*

*To Megan,*

*one of my biggest encouragers.*

*I can't count the times she asked,*

*"How is book 3 going?"*

*My God is amazing.*

*He has a way of putting me into situations*

*I would never put myself into.*

*I always come out finding a purpose behind it.*

"Don't worry about anything; instead, pray about everything. Tell God what you need, and thank him for all he has done.  Then you will experience God's peace, which exceeds anything we can understand. His peace will guard your hearts and minds as you live in Christ Jesus.

And now, dear brothers and sisters, one final thing. Fix your thoughts on what is true, and honorable, and right, and pure, and lovely, and admirable. Think about things that are excellent and worthy of praise.  Keep putting into practice all you learned and received from me—everything you heard from me and saw me doing. Then the God of peace will be with you."

(Philippians 4:6-9) NLT

When life gets busy, it's easy to worry.  In the middle of life, just give it to God and you will be less stressed and have a real chance at peace.

# Time Difference Reference

T ime Difference Reference

| Zelle | = | Jareneiks (Deltik) |
|---|---|---|
| 1 month | = | 1 year |
| 15 days | = | 6 months |
| 5 days | = | 2 months |
| 1 day | = | 12 days |
| 2 hours | = | 1 day |
| 1 hour | = | 12 hours |
| 5 min | = | 1 hour |
| 1 min | = | 12 min. |

Dear Reader,

I am not big on Author Notes. I will be honest, I rarely read them. This book is a little different. It is from two different points of view. It starts off from Jahni's point of view like the first two books, and then switches to her younger brother, Jon's point of view. I have no intention of leaving you guessing on who is telling the story... so to make it a little simpler, Jon or Jahni will be written under the chapter heading.

I pray you have a blessed day and blessed life. Keep reading. God is great about talking us through any situation as long as we are willing to listen.


*Heidi Harris*

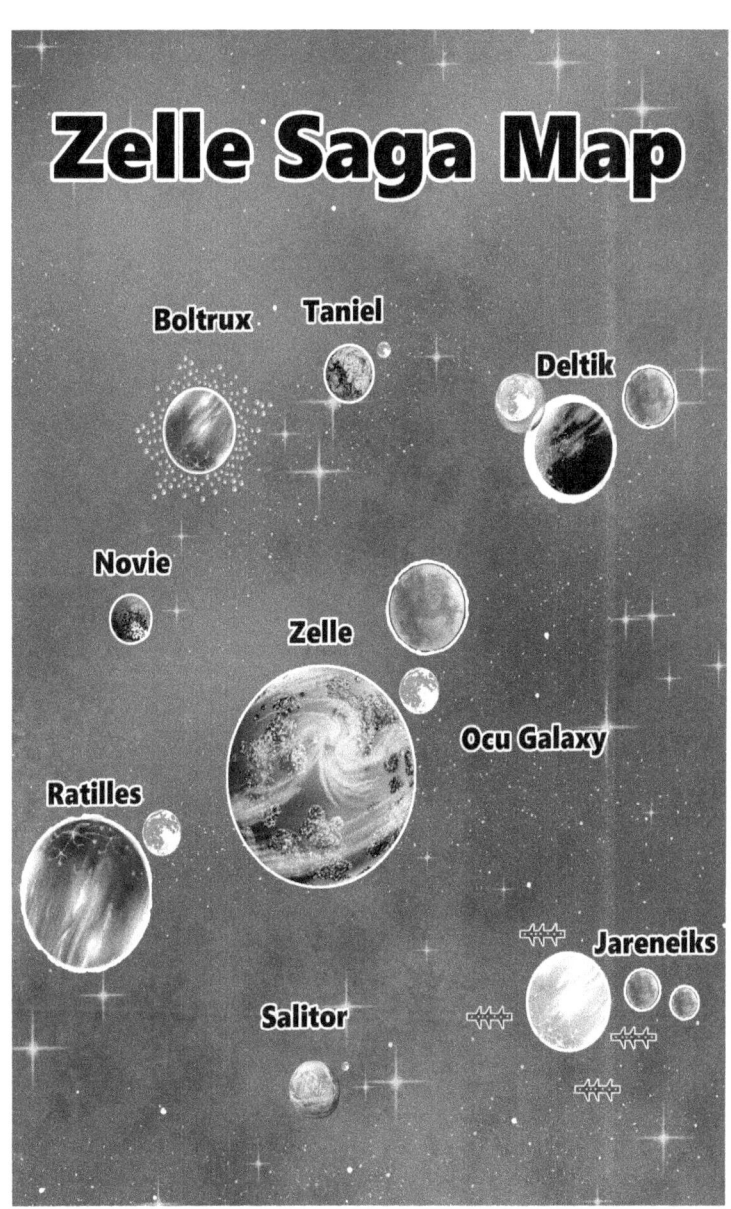

# PROLOGUE

(Jahni)

I was back on MaCownia. Dirt whipped around with the wind and slapped me in the face. The smell hit me next. I gasped for air and tried to step away from it, but my back hit a wall. I groaned and darted toward the next exit. I walked into an empty white hallway. I was caught off-guard when I saw my brother through the one-way glass. He had one hand on the table and the other on his lap.

"Jon!" I called his name.

He couldn't hear me. I searched frantically for a door and couldn't find one. I had to get to him. I walked around the corner. I stopped in my tracks. I saw Rose behind another one-way glass. She was inside of a shack sitting on a dirty couch. She looked like she was more frustrated than anything.

Jon crawled off the floor and joined her on the couch. I pounded on the glass. Neither of them heard me. How did Jon get over there anyway? I backtracked to where I had seen him around the corner. He was still sitting in the same chair in the same position.  The door flew open, and Rose barged in and threw her arms around Jon's neck.  Jon protested.

I tried to make sense of what I was seeing.  My eyes fluttered open, and I left the dream behind.  Sloane was still asleep.  I spent the next thirty minutes in prayer.  Jon, Rose, Sloane, and I had a trip planned off world next week.

# 1

(Jahni)

"Remind me, why do we do this?" I asked my husband, thinking about the full week of work we both put in.

[Because,] He kissed my forehead. [we like to have this time together and we can't justify it if we don't work hard every day.] He was very convincing.

I heard a knock at the door. Our bubble shattered, and we were back in our room. I rolled my eyes. I am usually thankful for Sloane's ability to transform me into another place, at least holographically, but I didn't like the interruptions.

[This better be important.] Sloane growled his thoughts at the door.

[It is. I promise.] The thought belonged to Japhen.

Japhen's job was to make sure we didn't overlook any obligations or laws. Japhen was sincere. I let out an aggravated sigh. It took only a second to throw on a robe. Sloane didn't bother moving. I opened the door.

Japhen was standing there dressed in his best suit. I knew

this, because it was his blue suit. Last month, he came in and told me his wife had given it to him for his birthday. He was holding a folder. I held back a groan. It had to be illegal to be bothered this time of night.

"I really am sorry to bother you this time of night." He apologized.

"What couldn't wait until tomorrow?" As a queen, I knew I had responsibilities, but if we were not in the middle of an attack, there was no reason to bother me at this time of night. For the most part, Zalnorel was a peaceful place to live.

"I know tomorrow is your day off, but tomorrow is Janghighns birthday and as I reviewed your schedules, I noted you had not accepted his invitation." Japhen's Trizmentes were getting more nervous with each word.

A Trizmente, also known as a Triz, reveals more than just a simple thought, but an actual feeling. I loved that about my species. I didn't have to wait for someone to spell out that they were sad. I could feel it. When I lived with the Jareneikians, I lived in oblivion.

"That is correct." Sloane's tone didn't hide his agitation.

"Is there a reason?" Japhen became more nervous.

Sloane's mouth went into a straight line. That was not a good sign for Japhen. Sloane almost never lost his temper, but Japhen was pushing him over the edge. I was almost there myself. It had been a ridiculous week with too many obligations and more paperwork than anyone deserved. I really needed some alone time with my husband.

"Yes." Sloane replied roughly.

Japhen finally noticed Sloane's Triz. He tumbled backward a step. He closed the folder and waited for a response.

"Dad will be attending on our behalf." I intervened before Sloane lost the remainder of his composure.

"Oh. I wish I knew that before I came here." Japhen apologized.

[Me too!] Sloane thought to me. To Japhen he said, "Next time leave a message, and use the Com Screen. We do not need to be bothered at this time of night unless it is a matter of life and death, okay?"

"Yes, sir." Japhen bowed out of the room and closed the door.

I jumped into bed and laughed. Sloane threw his head back onto the pillow. I put my hand on his chest and snuggled closer.

"What was he thinking?" Sloane shook his head in disgust.

"I really don't know." I kissed him on his chest. "I bet he won't do that again."

"I hope not." Sloane pulled me closer and kissed me.

# 2

(Jahni)

"Today is the day." Dad smiled at us.

"It is." Sloane agreed.

[I expect a communication from you every day.] Dad told Jon and Rose.

"Yeah yeah." Jon shook his head. [You stay on that Jahni.]

I laughed. [Fine.]

Dad caught us. "Jon, that means you too."

Jon let out a heavy breath. "Whatever you say."

"That's a yes." Rose chirped.

Jon shook his head, and mouthed no at me over Rose's shoulder, so Rose couldn't see him and Dad wouldn't sense we were talking. I laughed. Rose turned around.

[What?] Jon thought innocently.

Rose's brows furrowed. [Don't do that.]

[Do what? Sister dear.] Jon batted his eyes and put his hands elegantly by his head.

[You're not fooling me, Jon Julian.] Rose glared.

Jon laughed and dropped the act. [I think Dad is trying to say something. Why aren't you listening?]

Rose sighed as if she had to deal with too much and she was the only one who could do it. Jon shook his head and leaned back against the couch. I refocused my attention on Dad. He had stopped to take the situation in.

"Who is in charge?" Dad asked.

"Jahni and Joe." Jon and Rose said together.

"And that means?" Dad asked.

"What they say goes." Jon answered.

"Do you go anywhere without your Wrist Com's?" Dad asked.

"No." Jon's tone was bland.

"We don't have WC's." Rose tilted her head. "Mine broke last week."

"You don't." Dad put a finger to his chin.

He walked over and pulled out a large bag from behind the chair. He handed a package to Rose with an orange flowered ribbon and a pink box. He handed Jon a package with several different Shuttle Cars on it. He handed me a lavender package that matched my eyes. He handed Sloane a red package.

Rose had her WC on her wrist in seconds. Jon was looking his over. I gently took mine out of the box and turned it on. A holographic projection of a woman appeared.

"Thank you for choosing WC for me! At Com Com or CC as we like to call it." She did a mock wink. "We hope you use your WC to the fullest. Now to click stealth mode, touch the number one." She pointed to the left side of the screen where a number one button lit up. "To continue using your WC loud and proud, go for number two." She indicated the right side of the screen. "To enjoy your WC loud and proud without eavesdroppers, plug in your cordless headphone adapter and place your listening device in your ear." She did the same with her WC. "For underwater listening, don't forget to buy our waterproof earpieces at the Com Com store. Not only are they super comfy, they keep the water out!"

The lady disappeared and the CC logo popped up. The short clicky beat played in the background of "Come down to the Com Com store."

"Thanks, Dad!" Rose threw her arms around his neck. "You're the best!"

"You're welcome." Dad laughed.

"Sweet." Jon whistled loudly. "I like it."

"Thanks Alex." Sloane grinned.

"I love it, Dad." I gave him a hug.

"Just remember to use it to contact me!" Dad laughed.

Sloane turned the box over to read the details. "Looks like

it is the latest model with waterproof capabilities."

"It goes on sale next month." Dad grinned.

Jon walked across the room to the Com. He placed the new WC by the Com. The screen lit up.

"Jon Julian." Jon told the Com.

The Com dinged. A box popped up. Password confirmed.

"Copy files." Jon gave the command.

"Files copied." The Com responded.

"Transfer files to WC." Jon ordered.

"Files transferred." The Com confirmed.

Jon grinned. Rose walked to Jon's side and transferred her files to her WC.

Jon swung his backpack over his back. "Ready." He proclaimed as he came down the stairs.

"A little help, please?" Rose looked directly at Sloane.

[Jahni, we are not taking all of that with us.] Sloane informed me.

I looked at the pile of bags and suitcases at the top of the stairs. It was more than enough for a year. I'm pretty sure I could fit into the large one comfortably.

"We can't take all of that." I told her.

"Rose, are you serious?" Jon asked when he looked at the pile.

"What?" She asked innocently. "I have to have my makeup and my hair stuff, not to mention my clothes." Rose complained.

"Rose, you're going to have to downsize." I told her. "If you can't carry it, you can't take it."

Rose threw her hands in the air and looked at Jon in exasperation. "How do we deal with these people?"

Rose turned around and marched back to her room, dragging a suitcase. I could hear her muttering to herself. Jon laughed and rolled his eyes.

"You should have me pack for her." Jon rubbed his hands together, and grinned.

"Yeah, but all you would have had was a spare tee-shirt and a pair of jeans." I wasn't sure it was with my husband or brother, but they rarely needed more than a backpack.

"Clean underwear!" Rose yelled

[Yeah, I would have got those too.] Jon cringed. [Maybe.]

I laughed.

[Don't laugh Jahni! He was serious.] Rose told me.

[Maybe.] Jon's grin was my confirmation that she was right.

Rose toted another bag back to her room. Jon picked up one of the smaller bags and tossed it in her general direction. It landed with a loud thwack.

I cringed. [She'll have a fit if that was breakable.]

"Jon! That better not be my makeup bag." Rose stomped out of her bedroom.

Jon shrugged and grinned unrepentantly. Rose looked at the bag at her feet. Apparently, it wasn't her 'valuables'.

"You're lucky it wasn't." Rose stood in Jon's face.

"You ready yet?" Jon smirked.

Rose glared and turned on her heels. She finally got her clothes and essentials down to a mere three bags.

"I can hold them…see." Rose demonstrated.

Sloane wasn't convinced and his right eyebrow went up in doubt. He looked so handsome, I couldn't help smiling. Sloane caught me staring and grinned. I grinned wider after I was caught staring.

"Here." Jon told Rose and took the largest bag from her.

"Thanks Jon, you're my favorite brother." Rose gleamed.

[Still your only brother.] Jon told her.

[That's one of the reasons you're my favorite.] Rose kissed his cheek and trotted down the stairs.

Sloane laughed.

"Shut up." Jon muttered to Sloane.

"Didn't say a word." Sloane grinned.

I took Sloane's hand, and we were on the ship when Rose came through the door. Rose put her bags in the back. Jon left his by the door. Sloane and I climbed into the front and took our seats.

We told Dad we would take Jon and Rose to as many of the 23 surrounding galaxies during their break as possible. It was going to be a challenge, but we were going to try to make it to each one. One way or another, it was going to be an interesting experience, of that I was sure. Dad waved from the front porch. We waved back, and then we were in the air crossing the outer atmosphere of our planet.

# 3

(Jahni)

"Wait until you see this." I grinned.

[What Jahni?] Jon asked offhandedly.

"Don't mind Jon." Rose rolled her eyes.

"I don't." Sloane smirked.

Jon rolled his eyes.

I watched the planet come into view. It was a pale color of purple and magenta. The surrounding space of the planet shimmered.

"What makes it shine?" Rose asked.

"Diamonds are hidden in the debris." Sloane answered.

"Diamonds!" Rose giggled. "Can we pick up some souvenirs, Jahni?"

I turned around just in time to see Jon roll his eyes again. I laughed. I shook my head no.

The Vaktow landed gently on top of the purple shrubbery. It was too fuzzy to be called grass. The readings on the Com deemed the air safe to breathe. The land and shrubs were safe to walk on. Most of the water was safe to drink as well. I appreciated the Com even more.

Rose popped open the door and walked out. Jon followed her, and I headed up the end. Sloane had taken his shortcut outside of the Shuttle Car. He grinned at me as he closed the door.

# 4

(Jon)

Rose spun around, dancing, and giggling. I shook my head at her. I bent down and touched the purple stuff under our feet.

[I never saw purple grass before, or whatever they're called.] I thought.

"It's not really grass." Jahni reminded me.

"That's right. What do they call it then?" I asked.

"Ralemantina." Sloane answered.

"Rali what?" [That's odd. I think I like purple grass better.] I commented.

"Ra lem an ti na." Jahni pronounced the word in syllables for me.

"Ralemantina. Ralemantina. Ralemantina." Rose exclaimed as she did a cartwheel. She followed that with a backflip, another cartwheel, and finished with a front flip.

"I'm impressed." Joe told her.

Rose spun around in a giggle. "Thank you."

"You think that's impressive." I told Joe.

I looked at my sister Rose. She looked at me. I felt a grin slide across my face.

"Show them?" Rose's look was mischievous.

"Yeah." I agreed.

We had been working on a routine for five weeks. There was a talent show at the end of the school year and we were planning on winning it. We still needed a song.

[I think I found the song.] Rose thought to me.

[Which one?] I asked.

Rose messed with the Com on her wrist as she walked over and stood beside me. The music started playing, and she spun into a handless front flip. At the same time, I spun into a handless backflip.

She went to her left in another handless front flip and I went to my right in another handless backflip. I spun into a frontward roll. Rose turned to her right and did four handless front flips. Her last flip went over top of me, rolling under her. I popped up. She did a backflip and turned it into a frontward roll. I did two backflips, turned it into three front flips, so the last front flip went over Rose in a roll.

Rose stood up. "Well, that's as far as we have gotten with that." She turned off the music.

Jahni and Joe both clapped for us. I took a bow. Rose did

a curtsy.

"Not bad, so far." I said.

"Not bad at all." Jahni grinned.

"Well, the talent show is coming up." I answered.

"I think you will win." Joe nodded his head.

I shrugged like I didn't care, but It meant a lot that he beleived in us. I probably wouldn't tell it to my brother-in-law, but Jahni didn't do too bad when she decided to marry him.

To Rose, I thought. [We better win.]

[What did you think of the song?] She asked.

[It's okay.] I answered.

[You mean it's perfect, right?] Rose asked.

[Sure.] I replied.

[I thought so too.] Rose beamed.

I wanted to [add a few martial arts moves. I'm sure we could pull off a few fake punches and make it look good.] I knew Rose heard my thoughts.

[We can do that.] Rose agreed.

[That was one thing I loved about my sister. She was up for anything. Sometimes she acted a little prissy about her clothes.] Rose heard me, but smiled.

"How did you talk him into doing that with you?" Joe asked.

"It wasn't hard." Rose crossed her arms and gave me a

mock challenge glare.

[That's because it was my idea.] I thought to Rose.

She let her arms drop. "Shh. I'm not telling them that part."

"Telling us what?" Jahni asked.

"Nothing." Rose said innocently and put on a grin.

"Uh huh." Joe looked from Rose to me.

"Let's go check out the planet." Jahni let us off the hook.

I grinned. [Jahni, you are the best.] I thought to my sister alone.

[Thank you. I think you are alright too.] Jahni grinned back.

"Okay." Joe agreed.

Jahni held out her hand to Joe, and we started off on our walk. Rose skipped the first few steps until she noticed I wasn't moving. She motioned me to join them.

"I'm coming." I huffed.

Most of our experience revolved around flowers and trees. On the plus side, I actually like hiking.

It wasn't long into our hike when we heard a big crash. The ground shook. Nothing seemed out of the ordinary.

"What was that?" Rose asked.

"I don't know." I searched around.

A strange white bird with three wings on either side flew

29

into the sky in a hurry. I had the distinct idea that they were trying to escape. Other birds followed them with a vengeance.

[Not a good sign.] I thought to Rose.

[No.] She agreed.

We all stopped in our tracks. The four of us looked at each other. The ground moved.

"Should we run?" Rose asked.

"Maybe." I said.

"I don't know." Jahni was just as baffled as we were.

"We need cover." Joe stated.

The ground shook more. The crash of trees was easy to hear. The birds were out of sight.

"Definitely." I agreed.

Before we could take off running, a beast the size of our Vaktow pushed his way into the clearing. We froze for a second. It's odd the things you notice in the midst of panic. The birds didn't move. The trees barely swayed with the breeze. Animals had vanished. The reality of death sunk in and we ran like our lives depended on it.

Whatever that beast was, he came fumbling after us. Joe took a hard left. The three of us followed his move. The beast tumbled as he tried to stop. The crash of the trees following was unmistakable. Feathers exploded into the air. The squeaks and squawks of the birds came next. Rose giggled at the sound of the birds.

Jahni put a finger to her lips. [We don't want to tell him where we are at.]

[Yeah, he might eat us.] I threw in.

Rose squeaked. She quickly covered her mouth with her hands. [Sorry.]

[I vote we leave this planet.] I thought.

[Ditto.] Rose confirmed.

[I agree with the twins.] Jahni thought to Joe.

[A bunch of sissies.] Joe shook his head and chuckled.

[Says the man who can pop away at any time.] I retorted.

[That's an idea.] Joe thought to us.

[What?] I asked.

[Using my abilities.] Joe answered.

[Now we're talking.] I thought back.

Joe projected an image of a deep river stretching between the beast and us. The beast looked incredibly confused. It sniffed the air and put a paw in the fake water. It brought the paw back to see it was dry. The beast growled.

The beast's eyes turned red and leapt into the air towards us. We raced to the edge of the cliff and slid down a large hill on our butts. We landed on flat ground and sprinted off. The beast roared at the top of the hill. It pounced into the air, coming straight for us. Rose screamed. We scrambled together.

Joe took Jahni's hand. Rose and I each touched his forearm. We were several yards away from the beast when we landed. Joe looked down at the foot of the hill. It wasn't large enough to be a mountain. We were standing at the base immediately.

A roar rang through the hillside. Rose shivered. Jon looked over his shoulder.

Joe's gaze was locked in the distance. We appeared where he had been looking. The Vaktow was within seeing distance.

[Thank God.] Jahni thought.

[Yeah.] Rose agreed.

The next thing I knew, we were on the Vaktow. Everyone sat down. Joe had it in the air in minutes.

"Well, that sucked." I kicked my legs up onto the corner of the Vaktow and leaned back into my seat.

"What? You don't want to go back?" Joe asked.

"Sure, isn't next month Fright Night? What do you say, Rose?" I grinned in Rose's direction.

Rose punched my arm. I laughed. Joe looked very amused.

"I guess that's a no for Rose." I laughed again.

"I don't know how you would know. Rose is so subtle." Jahni grinned.

"Oh, I can read in between the lines." I winked at Rose.

"You think you're funny." Rose told me.

"I am." I grinned.

Rose rolled her eyes. "Joe's not the only one who lives in a delusional world."

"Hey!" Joe responded.

"Sorry Joe." Rose laughed.

"I think we can take her." I leaned forward and grinned wickedly.

"I was just kidding." Rose protested.

Joe turned the Vaktow on autopilot. He stood up and crossed his arms. Rose gulped.

"Just kidding?" Joe asked in a deep voice.

I chuckled. Joe nodded at me. I got out of my seat. Joe and I held her down and tickled her.

[Stop! Stop! I'm going to pee my pants.] Rose complained.

Joe and I stopped tickling her and laughed hysterically. Jahni was grinning from the front seat.

"Jahni!" Rose exclaimed, and brushed her hair back with her fingertips.

"Be smarter next time, or they will team up on you again." Jahni laughed.

"Fine. Only make one of them mad at me at a time. Got it." Rose grinned.

Jahni laughed. I rolled my eyes. Joe was back at the controls.

"I'm hungry." I told them.

[You're always hungry.] Rose thought to me.

"Food is in the back." Joe said.

"Sweet." I got up and went to the back of the Vaktow.

I popped open the seat and pushed the button on the wall for the door to the storage area to open. I headed straight for the fridge. It was tucked back in the corner, all 5 feet in height and 1 foot wide of it.

I opened the door and leaned in. I saw a bag of pizza bites. That would do. I grabbed them and threw them into the microwave. I took a plate full back to my seat. Rose reached for one.

"The first one is free. After that, get your own." I told her.

She rolled her eyes and reached for another. I jerked the plate away. Mess with a man's food and die. That was the law of the land on any planet. She should know that by now.

"I will make more." Rose growled.

"You better." I shared the plate. I was holding her to her word.

"Okay, so should we try another planet today?" Joe asked.

"Dinner on this planet?" I asked.

"Told you." Rose sighed dramatically.

"Home is about two hours away." Jahni added.

"We'd arrive about dinner time." Joe suggested.

"Do it." I agreed, as my stomach growled again.

# 5

(Jahni)

"What? Home after one day?" Dad smiled.

"Nice to see you too." Jon grinned.

"Someone was hungry." Rose gave Jon a pointed look.

"What?" Jon said in mock innocence.

"We were only a few hours from home." Sloane said.

"Sleeping in our own beds sounded like a good idea." I told him.

Dad laughed. "I'm glad you did."

Jon headed for the kitchen. [I'll let Salaranda know we're home.]

[Me too.] Rose raced after him.

"Everything go okay?" Dad asked once they left the room.

"Not exactly." Sloane winced.

"What happened?" Dad asked as his concerned Triz flowed openly toward us.

"We landed on Wayr." I paused.

"Yes, the one with the diamonds." Dad said.

I nodded in agreement. "We were hiking and a large beast started chasing us."

"We got away." Sloane added.

"I see." Dad's voice lowered an octave. "Do you want to call the quits?"

"No sir, we said we would make the trip and we plan to make the trip." Sloane's voice was sure.

Dad nodded and patted Sloane on the back. "Let's see if Salaranda is getting a meal together. I'm hungry too." Dad winked.

"Sounds good." Sloane agreed.

I entered the kitchen first. Jon and Rose were eating from a large bowl. Salaranda was popping a pan into the oven. She turned around and smiled.

"How was your trip?" Salaranda asked us eagerly.

Sloane laughed.

"Ut oh, that bad." Salaranda responded.

I laughed too. "No, it's going good. It's just on pause. We missed your good cooking."

Salaranda smiled. "Good, too many leftovers when you four aren't around."

Dad laughed. "Apparently, I haven't been eating enough."

Jon held up an empty bowl. "What are you trying to say?"

The timer went off and Jon jumped up, but Salaranda beat him to the stove. Dad laughed harder.

"I don't think I have to say anything, son." Dad patted him on the back.

"I'm a growing boy." Jon grinned.

"A growing stick, you mean." Rose teased.

"At least I am growing. You stopped." Jon threw back.

"I'm perfect just the way I am." Rose twirled to prove it.

"Yes, you are." I chimed in.

# 6

(Jon)

"Day two." I sat down at the table.

Dad flicked off the Com on the wall. "You coming home for supper?"

I rolled my eyes. "Stop grinning like that."

"Fine." Dad kept grinning.

"Maybe we will. What of it?" I asked.

Dad laughed. "Nothing. I'm glad you did."

Rose floated into the room, grinning. "I had the best dream."

"Cool." I said.

"What about?" Jahni asked as she walked into the room.

"I can't tell!" Rose grinned. "If I tell, it won't come true."

"Rose, it's not a wish." I answered.

"The rules still apply!" Rose was vehement.

"Whatever makes you feel better?" I grumbled.

"Feel better? Is someone sick?" Salaranda was

concerned.

"No one's sick." Dad responded.

"Oh, good." Salaranda put a hand to her chest in relief and left the room to get another tray.

"Have you been to Grek?" Dad asked.

"No." Joe walked into the room.

"Grek would be fun. I love their beaches." Jahni took her seat.

"So it's warm?" Rose asked.

"It was the last time we went." Jahni grinned at Joe.

"I could stand some warmth. My tan does need a little help." Rose held up her arm and examined it thoroughly.

"To get a tan, you actually have to spend time in the sun." I told her.

"I do when it's warm out. All it has been doing is raining. Who wants to be out in that?" She told us dramatically and then laughed at herself.

"The Zanxtear Race is coming up soon." Joe smiled.

"I'll be ready." I told him confidently.

"Are you moving up to the Senior Division this year?" Joe tried to keep a straight face.

"Not planning on it." I responded.

"You could go either way. If you do Junior another year, you have a good chance of placing first this time." Jahni commented.

"That's true." I agreed.

"But if you move up to the Senior Division, you have to go up against Joe and Jasmine." Rose threatened.

"The dynamic duo." Jahni smiled.

"Yeah. We got first and second. You're welcome to third." Joe grinned.

The Zanxtear Race was a big thing on Zelle. If you were fast enough and smart enough, you had a good chance at winning. Interviews followed, as well as publicity. Jaz was princess of Landryn and didn't need to be publicized. Uncle Adeam was doing his best to keep her out of the papers. Joe was King of Zalnorel, so he didn't need it either. If he wanted an interview, he could have it at a moment's notice.

Although, because of his experience in the Zanxtear Race, he was rapidly ascending Alenworth, the Gaming Company of the planet. They designed everything from games on the Com, to Vaktow control consoles, to experimental sciences that would allow us to travel further and faster into surrounding galaxies.

Jahni was busy running a fair amount of Zalnorel. Dad was the people schmoozer aka he could talk most people into anything. Joe was working on advancing military possibilities, figuratively and practically.

I didn't have a clue what I was going to do when I was

expected to make a choice. Dad and Jahni never asked me to consider my future occupation. You would think it would have been decided for me at this point. Part of me was sure that would be easier. Jahni was not going to force me into something I didn't want. She thought it was better if I had options and Dad agreed with her. She had hated the lack of options she had with the Jareneikians.

I liked working with my hands, running, swimming, but I couldn't think of a career worth pursuing. I wasn't as smart as Jahni, nor was I as happy about stuff like Rose. Joe had a knack for fixing problems. What did I have?

Okay, too much thinking. I shook my head and decided that my life could wait a few more years before I had to figure it out. God would give me an answer then.

*Right God?* I asked cautiously.

*I have the perfect job in mind. It won't be easy and you won't expect it, but you are the man I will choose to do it.*

*Crap.* My head sunk. This should make it easier, but somehow it seems worse than not knowing if I had a place in my future. *What kind of job?*

*You can be a people schmoozer too.*

*Me? Have you met me? I say the wrong things half of the time. I mean, they cry...how is that going to accomplish anything?*

*Some people like and appreciate the direct sarcastic approach.*

*Okay, I can do that.* I felt peace cover me. I can be myself and fulfill God's purpose. I smiled.

"What are you smiling about?" Rose asked.

"Nothing." I told her. [Just contemplating the future.]

Rose nodded and accepted my answer without asking any questions.

"It's about time to start training for the race." Dad reminded us.

"It is." Joe grinned at me.

"I don't care about the dumb race. I just want to see the sun again. Let's go to Grek." Rose said.

"Do they have a beach? I'd like to do some surfing." I asked.

Jahni looked at Joe. "I think they do?" Jahni asked Joe.

"A beach would be fun." Joe agreed.

"Did you kids pack clothes for the beach?" Dad asked.

"Nope." I answered.

"Good thing we came home." Rose cheered.

"We'll grab some towels out of the closet." Jahni added.

"Grek it is." Joe smiled.

# 7

(Jon)

The snow began to fall. Rose hugged her shoulders. I saw my breath leave my mouth and puff out in a cloud that looked like smoke.

"Store." Jahni looked at Joe.

"Looks like." Joe agreed.

"What happened to paradise?" I asked.

"Winter." Joe grinned.

Joe took Jahni's hand, sprinted across the street, and flew into the nearest store with clothes in the window. Rose beat me inside.

[It's not that bad.] I shrugged as I closed the gaping door.

[Not in here.] Rose answered.

Jahni and Joe were several aisles overlooking at the winter merchandise. Rose stood on her tiptoes, so she could see better. A smile lit her face when she saw something she liked and ran off. I shrugged again and headed towards men's clothing. I pulled a blue coat off the rack and put it on. The coat fit perfectly. I pulled it off and headed to the counter. I pulled out the appropriate bills and handed them to the cashier. She smiled and handed me back the change.

"Did you find everything already?" Jahni asked.

"Yep." I held the jacket up for her to see.

"Rose is going to be awhile." Jahni giggled.

I followed Jahni's gaze. Rose was holding up an outfit and looking in the mirror. She shook her head no and picked up another. I chuckled too.

"Sloane and I are heading to the back of the store." Jahni said. "You okay here?"

"I'll survive." I answered.

Jahni walked away with Joe. Finally, I gave up waiting on Rose to get done shopping and walked over to the window ledge and sat down. I turned on my WC and enabled 3D images.

It popped up about 3 inches in either direction. I froze the frame so it would stay in place when I moved my wrist. I tapped the top of my WC and it returned to stealth mode. I widened the image and opened ME aka Mysterious Exploration. It was an adventure game. My character was named JJ after me for Jon Jr. JJ got out of bed and stretched. JJ exited the house.

JJ got on his bike. Dust flew into the air as he sped away. A woman was by the side of the road. I froze in time while she asked a question: *Could you give me a lift?*

Another box popped up. *Accept quest or Deny quest.* I tapped on accept. She climbed on the bike. When we got to town, she gave me a bag full of cash. It was just enough to assist me in my fourth long quest. I took JJ to the center of town. We entered the Exploration Hub. I went up to the Hub Master.

A screen popped up: *Do you wish to accept a quest? Another screen popped up. Accept or Deny quest.* I tapped accept. A screen popped up. *Congratulations! Quest #4 is in the next kingdom. You must climb Tatha Mountain and find the flower of healing.* A picture of a pink flower with purple leaves popped up on the screen. Another box popped up. *Beware of the Farflex guarding the flower. Watch out for frozen icicles that come from the Farflex's mouth. You will need to buy a shield and defensive weapons. Good luck!*

The box faded. I took JJ to the store to buy a shield. I chose a sword, and a set of throwing knives. JJ climbed on the bike. Dust flew in the air. The sun was declining. JJ would be forced to spend the night somewhere.

Rose hit my arm. I jerked to attention. She was holding a full store bag.

"What?" I paused the game and saved it.

"We're done." Rose modeled her new outfit.

"Okay." I closed my game down, and it disappeared. I put on my coat and stood up. Jahni and Joe were waiting by the door.

[What is there to do on this planet besides shopping?] I grumbled.

"Who cares? Shopping is fun." Rose spun around and caught a snowflake in her mouth. "Mmm, the snow tastes like candy!"

"Seriously?" I asked.

Joe was pushing buttons on his Com. "The Com says it's safe to eat."

I opened my mouth and caught a small snowflake. A sweet piercing taste hit my tongue. I wanted more. The snowflakes were too small to satisfy my taste buds. I walked over to the nearest snowdrift and cupped my hands together, and gathered the snow into my hands to eat.

"Ooo." Rose complained.

[What, it's good.] I told her.

"Do you know where that's been?" Rose asked.

"Don't care." I answered and licked the snow.

Rose's nose scrunched up in disgust. "I don't understand you sometimes."

[That makes two of us.] I thought.

[I heard that.] Rose complained.

[Still don't care.] I answered.

"Alright, what do you want to do in Snow Village?" Joe

asked.

"Sorry guys." Jahni bit her bottom lip.

"It's okay, Jahni." Rose squeezed her hand.

"I guess. We can find another warm planet." I took a shot at encouraging her.

"But we promised you the sun." Jahni laughed.

"Big promise." I laughed. [Everything doesn't always go well.] "It's fine. Really it is. I got to start the fourth quest on my game." I told her.

"So it wasn't so bad waiting around for Rose to finish shopping." Jahni grinned.

I shrugged. "Can we go snowboarding or something?" I asked.

"I don't see why not. Let's go ask someone." Jahni agreed.

We walked into the nearest building. It was a restaurant. Joe went up to the counter and asked if there was a place to go skiing or snowboarding. I overheard him giving Joe directions.

He came back. "It's not that far away. Do you want to go now or later?"

"Now." Rose and I said together. We both laughed.

"You know you're going to lose." I told them with no humility.

I may not be good at everything, but I could snowboard.

All three of them would be eating snow if I had anything to do with it. The snow was delicious, so I didn't feel bad at the prospect of demolishing them.

"Not if I beat you." Rose grinned.

"You didn't last time." I reminded her.

"It's a new day, new possibilities." Rose adjusted her hat as if daring me to beat her.

I laughed at her antics. She was funny. At least she wasn't complaining about the change in scenery. One of these dumb planets had to be in summer.

"Perfect fit." Rose grinned.

Ditto. Nothing worse than loose snow boots. Okay, maybe one or two things are worse. Going for a swim right now in this cold weather would definitely be worse. Facing down a hungry animal might be another. I thought about the beast from Wayr.

"You're going to lose this time." Rose put on her game face.

"In what century?" I asked her.

"This one, cause you're so going down." Rose's nose scrunched up.

I chuckled. "Whatever makes you feel better."

Jahni finished putting her gear on and we headed to the slopes. We took a seat on the lift and headed to the top.

"It's a long way down." Jahni said.

"I got you." Joe reassured her.

"Part of the excitement in life is the fall. If there is no risk, what's the fun?" Rose grinned.

"No risk in this. If I fall, I will just snowboard my way down." I winked.

"Sure you will." Rose laughed.

We reached the top. Rose and I got out first. Jahni and Joe got off after us.

A few people were fumbling around on their skis and snowboards. I grinned. It was a nice feeling to know I had this under control. The four of us took our positions. The cold air hit my face. Instead of making me cold, I felt exhilarated. Rose's cheeks were glowing pink.

"Are you ready?" Joe asked.

"Absolutely." Rose pulled down her glasses.

"When you are." I returned.

[We'll see.] Jahni thought.

"Ready...set...go!" Rose yelled.

We took off. I didn't go very fast at first. Slowly, I gained speed. I bent down to gain the momentum I was looking for. The hills started within the first minute.  It wasn't the tallest slope.  It wasn't the smallest either.  I was in the lead and planning to keep it.

The finish line was in sight.  I buckled down my heels and aimed for it.  I curved my snowboard into a stop.  Jahni came in a close second.  I thought I would be racing Joe down the hill, but my sister was surprisingly good.

"Congratulations."  Joe grinned at Jahni.

"Thank you."  Jahni grinned and leaned forward for a kiss.

"Hey, what about me?"  I complained.

[You're the one who said you would win.  I don't think that deserves a Congratulations.]  Rose tried to get a rise out of me.

[How was last place?]  I countered.

[Whatever.]  Rose rolled her eyes.

"You want a kiss too."  Joe grinned.

"No."  I rolled my eyes.

"I'll take one."  Rose pointed to her cheek.

Joe chuckled and kissed her on the cheek.

"Kissing two beautiful women in the same night.  I should tell your wife."  Jahni retorted.

"Can I convince you to keep it between us?"  Joe closed in on Jahni and wrapped his arms around her.

"I don't know.  It can be fun to watch a man squirm."

Jahni pretended to be thoughtful.

"That's not right." Joe told her seriously.

Jahni leaned forward and kissed him. A few people stopped and laughed before they walked away. I rolled my eyes.

"What were we talking about again?" Joe asked.

"The slopes." I threw in.

I was tired of watching them flirt. I wanted to get back up there. I had a rep to protect, and I planned on winning every trip we made down each hill.

"Round two. Round two." Rose cheered.

"Okay. Okay." Jahni agreed.

It wasn't long before we were at the top again. We were going to hit each trail three times. At least that had been the plan when I started getting hungry. We had only been at it for two hours. I slid into the finish line. I had lost count of how many times I had beat them. Jahni had come close a few times, but I maintained my score.

"Loser buys food, right?" I asked.

Joe exhaled. He had come in last.

"I'm kind of hungry too." Rose helped me.

"What about it, Sloane?" Jahni winked.

"Sure. I guess." Joe said, followed by the grumbling of his stomach.

"Real hard to talk you into that one." I grinned.

"I never said I wasn't hungry too." Joe stepped off the snowboard.

Jahni laughed. "Come on, boys." She detached herself from the snowboard, looped her arm around Joe's waist, and trotted off with the snowboard in her free hand.

Rose and I raced to catch up. We made our way to the slope restaurant. I couldn't read the name, but I could smell the food.

The food started coming. The four of us stopped and looked at each other. Rose let out a big sigh and put her hands together.

"I'll do it." Rose said.

The rest of us bowed our heads and listened to her prayer. I resisted the urge to peek at the food as I waited. My stomach was thoroughly growling. I added my silent thanks to God as Rose finished saying the prayer.

"This is the best Jahni. It's been forever since we have been to the slopes." Rose oozed.

"Three months." I corrected her.

She didn't even bat an eye as she continued. "I don't even mind falling in the snow when it tastes so delicious."

Jahni laughed. "I'm glad you are enjoying yourself."

[Okay, I'll admit it.] "I'm having fun too." [It's nice to crush you guys coming down the hill.] I grinned.

"Hey." Rose complained.

I chose to ignore her. "But really Jahni, I want an adventure. And when I say adventure, I mean beaches and surfing. I want to swim so much I feel waterlogged. I don't care what planet we have to go to get there."

"Okay, beach...got it." Jahni grinned.

"Now we can continue with our pit stop until the real adventure." Joe rolled his eyes and then winked at us.

"I do want to go for a swim." Jahni snuggled up close to Joe.

At least my sister was using her powers for good. I could almost feel the sun on my skin now. Joe almost always let Jahni have her way.

"I'll keep that in mind." Joe grumbled and put an arm around my sister's shoulder and pulled her closer.

"How many more galaxies do we have left?" Rose asked as she poked a fork into her dessert.

"We haven't even been to half of them." I told her.

"I could figure that out by myself." Rose shook her head in disgust.

"A lot." Joe smirked.

"A lot, a lot." Jahni agreed with Joe.

Rose giggled. "Okay, I see a theme."

"Let's see…About 20 more to go to." Joe answered.

"What!" Rose exclaimed. "We've been to like…how many planets?" Rose looked at me.

I shrugged. I could count them up, but I didn't feel like wasting the mind power to do so. Rose turned her attention back to Joe.

"But we have been to at least five planets." Rose protested.

"Yes, planets." I agreed. [Three of them were to fuel up, so it wouldn't count even if it were galaxies.]

"Oh." Rose's head drooped when she realized what I meant. "We're never going to finish this in the next twelve days."

Jahni and Joe laughed. I hadn't given it much thought, but it would be ridiculous to assume you could enjoy each galaxy in less than a day. All I had heard was space-trip.

"That does mean more field trips." Rose was all sunshine as she took a bite. She leaned her head on her hand and spun her other hand with the fork in the air and took a second bite.

Jahni chuckled. "I make no promise until I see the end of this one."

"Oh, don't give me that Jahni. I'm sure we can talk you into another one. No matter how badly this one ends up." Rose wiggled her eyebrows.

I busted out laughing. I thought it was hilarious. Jahni simply shook her head and decided now was the best time to eat her food. It wasn't too long after that we were done eating.

"More slopes?" I asked eagerly.

"My legs are already hurting." Rose told me point blank.

I shrugged. "It's not my fault if you've been a lazy bum."

"Lazy! I'm not remotely lazy." Rose protested.

I shrugged again.

"Don't give me that." Rose lowered her eyes at me.

"So you're up for it?" I asked.

Rose huffed. "Fine."

"You two are very entertaining." Jahni told us.

"We try." I grinned smugly.

Rose shook her head. We headed up the lift again and sailed down the slope quickly. I even got a few jumps in. Rose was playing it safe. Jahni wasn't trying to outdo me, but she was keeping up.

It was two more hours before we decided to call the quits. We stayed in the Slopes Inn. Rose and I shared a room. I took the bed closest to the door. I fell into bed and didn't know anything for the next eight hours.

# 8

(Jon)

The Vaktow door opened.  The smell of the ocean breeze hit my face before I saw the ocean.  When I did see the ocean, I was not disappointed.  It stretched as far as I could see.

[Yes!]  I thought.

[I'm psyched too.]  Rose agreed.

"Now this is what I'm talking about."  I gave Jahni a high five.

"I thought we needed a day in paradise after planet blizzard."  Jahni grinned at my surprise.

"Good choice."  I told her.

I leaned over the seat and grabbed my backpack.  I swung it over my shoulder.  I took off in a sprint straight for the ocean.  I pulled my shirt over my head and threw onto the sand.  I stepped out of my shoes and tucked the socks inside.  Within seconds, my feet were hitting the sand.

I unzipped my backpack and found my swim trunks.  I let

the bag fall onto the sand. I looked around for a good spot to change.

[Personally, I didn't care if I changed right here on the beach. Rose would throw a fit if I did that again.] I let her hear my thoughts.

"Yep!" Rose complained. "Last time I had to go to therapy for three months!"

"Sure you did." I told her.

Rose had never been to therapy a day in her life. She was the most content person I knew. We argued and poked at each other, but it was mostly for sport. Nothing serious.

"Okay, it was a class on therapy. But that counts, right?" Rose admitted.

"Yeah, it counts." Joe agreed. "I would need therapy too."

"Shut up." I let my voice go down an octave to sound menacing.

I turned on my heels and headed for a clump of trees. It would do the trick. I slid off my jeans and boxers and pulled on the trunks. I wadded up the pile of clothes and made my way back. I slid the wad into my backpack, picked the shirt up from the sand, and put the shirt on top.

I dove into the water. I felt like it had been years. I loved the feeling of the water touching my body. I put one hand in front of the other and set a rhythm. Before I knew it, I could barely see the shoreline. I stopped and took it all in for a minute.

It was decision time. Could I swim out further and still make it back to the beach? I looked in both directions. I was sure I could see something further out. Curiosity got the best of me and I made an executive decision to pursue it.

My first instinct was to swim as fast as I could until I covered the distance. But on the off chance I was wrong, I wanted to make it back to shore, and going full speed ahead wouldn't help with my endurance. The closer I got, I was sure it was green. Possibly a small island in the middle of this vast ocean. It was still too soon to tell.

There was a very thin line of landmass from where I had approached the water. It was in that moment that I realized I was too far out for my sisters or Joe to hear my thoughts. I shook off what their worried reactions would be when I returned. I'd deal with that grief when I got back.

For now, I was too close to my goal. My limbs were exceedingly tired, and I needed to rest. Keeping the saltwater out of my mouth had been a trial in itself. My lips were burning and splitting down the middle.

It took me a lot longer than I had originally anticipated. The large stretch of water made everything seem closer when it was much further away. I couldn't see the shore I had come from anymore, but I had a good sense of direction and knew exactly which way to go. I closed in on the island. The trees appeared to grow before me.

I pulled myself onto my feet. I shook my arms. They were exhausted. The burn would feel good tomorrow. I walked towards the beach, wading through the water longer than I would have liked.

I crawled onto the shore. The wet sand felt good on my chest. I used my arm for a pillow. Exhaustion took over, and I passed out.

The next thing I knew, Joe was shaking me awake. My eyes flew open. I jumped to my feet, startled. My arms hurt. At first I wondered why and then I remembered I had just swam further than I had in my life.

"Aren't you going to say anything?" I demanded.

"Why bother, you wouldn't listen." Joe smirked. "Besides, between Jahni and Rose, you will never hear the end of it."

My shoulders slumped. "How long have I been asleep?" I asked.

Joe shrugged. "Hard to tell. You have been gone for three hours."

I winced. "They are going to kill me."

"If you're lucky, that's all they'll do." Joe grinned.

I groaned. "Where are they?"

"By the shore. I convinced them I could cover more ground on my own. You need to remember to charge your WC." Joe tapped my wrist.

"I thought I did." I looked down at my Wrist Com. It didn't look waterlogged, which was a good sign, but it was dead.

"Let's go." Joe told me.

"No." I answered.

"Huh?" Joe was puzzled.

"I know I'm dead, and I haven't even explored this island yet. If they are going to kill me, I want it to be for something." I explained.

Joe rolled his eyes and disappeared. Rose and Jahni stood before me seconds later. Joe found a tree to lean on as he watched both Rose and Jahni explode at me.

"What were you thinking?" Rose yelled.

"Where have you been?" Jahni demanded.

[Fell asleep.] I thought, although I was sure they couldn't hear me.

"We've never been on this planet; you could have been dead for all we know?" Rose tore into me.

"You can't go off by yourself." Jahni's voice was a magnified version of her normal volume.

It was pointless to say a word when they were like this.

The veins in Rose's forehead protruded, and it was all I could do not to make a joke. Explosions are great as long as they're not in your face.

"What's the point of a Wrist Com, if you can't use it?" Jahni asked.

"Dead." I managed to say something.

"Well, that explains one thing." Rose crossed her arms and glared.

"Someone needs to go with you." Jahni clarified on her earlier statement.

"Say something." Rose demanded.

Okay, me talk. "I'm sorry."

"Sorry he says." Rose growled and tears fell down her cheeks. Her body shook.

Oh, great. I stepped closer. What was I supposed to do about the tears? I think I like the exploding in my face thing better. I put my arms around Rose. She tried to shake me off at first, and then she began to sob and held me tighter than she had in her life.

Guilt weighed on me. [I didn't think they would make this big of a deal out of it.]

"Of course it's a big deal. We didn't know what happened to you. We were worried." Jahni's voice softened.

More guilt. I sagged beneath the pressure. Rose finally

let me go.  Joe decided to come into the conversation.

"Joe put a hand around Jahni's waist.  "He fell asleep."

"I didn't mean to…" I apologized.

"But you did."  Rose interrupted.

"Fell asleep?"  Jahni asked.

I nodded fervently.  Jahni sighed and held in her anger.
Rose was not so calm.  Her Triz were a straight jacket around my
body.

"Promise me, not to do that again."  Jahni's voice sank.

I put my right hand on my heart.  "I will never swim
across an ocean without telling someone again."

"That's not exactly what I meant."  Jahni told me.

I gave a cheesy grin.  "Forgiven?"

"Possibly."  Jahni countered.

"I don't think so."  Rose crossed her arms.

"I didn't mean to make you worry."  I tried again.  I had to
soothe things over before I asked my next question.

"You might not be leaving my side for a long time."  Rose
threatened.

"That could get a little awkward."  I shuttered.

Joe laughed.  "Yeah, maybe a little space is okay."

Rose's lips puckered together.  [Do not scare me again.]

[I can't promise that.]  I told her.

[But you can try.]  Rose persuaded.

[We'll see.] That was the best I could do.

[I'll take that as a yes.] Rose's mood lightened a little.

"Let's get out of here." Jahni looked at Joe.

"Can we at least explore the island first?" I asked them.

Rose was very defensive. I put on a fake smile of hope. Jahni sighed.

"Cut the kid some slack. He didn't realize everyone was worried." Joe cut into the conversation.

A flash of decision went through Jahni's eyes. "Yeah. We can explore."

[Thanks Joe.] I thought to my brother-in-law.

[You can owe me one.] Joe winked.

[Yeah.] I gave a nod.

"I guess we should get started." Jahni was getting antsy standing around doing nothing. She was always busy and wasn't used to staying put for very long.

I wasn't sure how big the island was. I liked having a backup plan. I wasn't hungry yet, but I would be soon. I have a ton of snacks in my backpack; the same one on the other side of the ocean. I hated to ask after Joe just bailed me out with my sisters, but realistically, he was the only one who could get there and back in less than a minute.

"I need my backpack." I looked at Joe hopefully.

Joe let out a groan. "You guys are more trouble than all

my money."

"You have a lot of money." Rose grinned.

Joe rolled his eyes and disappeared. He came back and dropped my backpack at my feet. I reached down and picked it up and slung it over my shoulder and grinned. I liked having it, in case I needed something. It was still daylight and was unlikely I would need my flashlight any time soon, but still...

I pushed back a tree branch and continued deeper into the island. The island sloped upwards. Mostly it was trees, rocks, and more sand. The further we climbed, the rockier it became. When we reached one of the peaks, I looked down, and saw a formation.

"What's that?" Jahni pointed.

"I don't know." Joe's right eyebrow lifted.

"It looks like words or one word." Rose speculated.

"It does." I agreed.

"Let's check it out." Jahni grinned.

"Absolutely." I smiled back.

This was more up my alley. Mysterious words on a concealed island. Okay, maybe not exactly concealed, but I did have to swim awhile to get here.

"Do you want a lift or the hard way?" Joe asked.

"Let's do a disappearing stunt. The scenic route would take forever." Rose told him.

Joe popped us down to the rocks. They were almost as tall as I was. I had kind of expected something bigger than pebbles, not the dark shiny blue boulders. At first, the boulders seemed black under the sun, but the navy blue was impossible to miss on further examination. The other rocks we had passed were made out of something else. I wondered what made them different.

"What does it spell?" Rose referred to the boulders.

[How am I supposed to know?] I thought back.

"Let me run it through the Wrist Com." Joe offered.

Joe pushed on his WC for a few minutes. He disappeared, and then he reappeared.

"I took a thermal scan. There is something underneath these rocks." Joe enlarged the diagram on his WC.

"Like what?" I asked.

Joe shrugged. "It appears to be the size of a large room."

"Tunnels?" Rose asked hopefully.

"Not that I can tell." Joe continued to fiddle with his Wrist Com.

There was a long pause in conversation. I took the moment to do a 360. A bird flew onto a nearby tree. It sang its heart out and another bird joined him. A leaf fell to my feet. The sun was directly above us.

"So where is the door at?" Rose looked at us eagerly.

"Find it and you'll know." I kicked up the sand.

"I want to, but where?" Rose poked the boulder and nothing happened.

"Some place that leads down." I chuckled.

Joe disappeared and reappeared on top of a boulder. He looked around. He disappeared again. While he was doing his hopping act, I decided to walk around. Every few feet, there was a gap. I walked around the boulder in front of me to see if I could find something. I didn't.

"Rose, stand on that side." I pointed to the other side of the boulder.

"Okay. Now what?" She asked.

"Ready, set, go!" I took off running and so did Rose. It wasn't long before Rose had lagged behind. [Jahni step out behind me.] I stopped running and turned around. I couldn't see her. [Jahni?]

[I'm looking right at you.] Jahni told me.

I turned around. [How did you get there?] She was standing directly in front of me.

I raced forward and Jahni appeared farther away. I stopped running. Rose came over and stood beside me.

[Walk that way.] I pointed to my west.

Jahni met us in the middle of the stones. Joe appeared beside Jahni. He tapped the WC.

[It's here.] Joe said.

"But where?" Rose asked.

"Walk straight." I suggested.

We put out our hands and walked forward. My hand bumped into something large. We surrounded it even though we couldn't see it. It was camouflaged by something. It made Jahni seem farther away like a mirror. Joe disappeared.

"It's not very tall." Joe offered.

"Can you walk through it?" Jahni asked.

"Give me a minute." Joe took a step into the object we couldn't see.

We heard a large creak, and a door opened. We still couldn't see what the door was connected to, but we could see what was inside it.

"Is it safe?" Rose was wary.

[Probably not.] I answered. "Let's do it."

Joe stood back for us to enter. We entered a large room. It had rock walls reaching twelve feet high. The rocks had been put together by someone to form this room. It had been hidden from outsiders as well. The question was, why.

Torches were laid by the front of the door. Rose reached down and picked them up. She examined the area and noticed something hanging on the wall. She pulled the large ring off the wall. At first, it looked like keys.

Rose rubbed both ends of the key like things together. A spark flew in the air. Rose grinned. It was flint and steel. It took her several times, but she lit the torch.

"Good guess." Jahni patted Rose on the back.

"I read it in a book once." Rose handed the torch to Jahni.

"Thanks." Jahni told Rose.

I didn't mention my flashlight in my bag. I let Rose have the win. Besides, any chance I could use fire, I was for it.

Joe was examining the walls and looking for another exit. It would be easier to look around if we had two torches lit, so I picked up another torch off the ground and handed it to Jahni. I put my torch to Jahni's. It lit instantly.

"Well, that takes all of the fun out of it." Rose shook her head in disgust.

I shrugged. "At least we have light now."

"What is this place?" Jahni walked over to Joe.

"Not sure. If I had to guess, I would say it was a safe house of some kind." Joe suggested.

"There is no water or food." Jahni responded.

"Exactly." Joe answered.

"Maybe they couldn't finish it." Rose offered.

"Unlikely." I muttered.

"So this is it?" Rose asked.

"I don't think so." Joe looked around carefully.

"What do you mean?" Jahni was confused.

"My WC is picking up an additional room underground. The question is, how do we get to it. I don't see any trapdoors in the floor." Joe explained.

"Ooo a hidden room." Rose skipped over to Jahni and Joe. "Let's find it."

Jahni held the torch next to the wall, so Joe could get a better look. The heat from the torches made writing and pictures appear on the walls. Joe started taking pictures and running it through a translator.

I walked over to the opposite wall. I leaned my torch up against the wall. Pictures and words appeared on it too. I wasn't familiar with the dialect, but it was of Ratillian descent. My stomach churned. I reminded myself that these caves were not active. The Ratillians couldn't find us here, but I was ready to leave. The hidden room no longer meant anything to me. I wished I had never seen this stupid island.

Jahni stood behind me. "What's wrong?" Her voice was gentle.

"We are standing in a Ratillian cave." My eyes were shut.

"But that's impossible." Rose sputtered.

I opened my eyes. "Look for yourself."

Rose examined the wall. She took a step back. The floor creaked beneath her weight. She looked down and was standing on the trapdoor.

"We have to see." Rose reached down to open the door.

I walked back to the entrance. "Nothing good can come from the Ratillians." I left the cave.

A big thud shut behind me. The door was gone. I felt against the hidden wall and felt no handle to open it.

[Joe, the door is shut.] I thought.

[I am trying to open it.] Joe replied.

Suddenly, the door flew open. I exhaled relief. I just wanted off this planet now.

"Come check this out!" Rose yelled.

Begrudgingly, I returned inside of the cave. Rose and Jahni had descended the stairs into the underground cavern. I slowly went down the stairs. It was glowing gold. Piles of barrels lined the walls. Several boxes lined the doorway.

Rose opened one of the boxes. "Wow!" Rose pulled out a ruby necklace.

She tossed a gold chain at my face. I caught it in my left hand. It had a lot of weight to it. My torch ducked down and warmed up the floor. Imprints of bodies lay on the floor. It gave me the creeps.

Rose saw it and froze. [Those are Ratillians.]

[It's only a picture.] I tried to reassure her.

"I don't need to see any more." Rose jumped up and left

the tunnel.

I grabbed the ruby necklace off the floor. Rose would want it later. I looked around the room and picked up two small boxes and carried them out.

Joe's WC beeped. The four of us were outside in the fresh air. It looked serene as the birds flew from tree to tree, chirping innocently.

[What does it say?] Jahni asked.

Joe grimaced. "It says: Here lies the last of the Ratillian forces. We will rise again and defeat our enemies. Those from Zelle will not survive."

Rose gulped. "How long ago was this?"

Joe tapped on WC. "Sixty years ago."

"I think it's time to leave this planet." Jahni put her hand on Joe's arm.

Joe nodded. He took us back to the beach in a few jumps. The sun still shone brightly. The sand was still amazing on my feet, but a torrent of anxiety had clouded all of it. We were on the Vaktow and leaving the horrible paradise.

"Let's get some rest before we try a new planet." Joe offered.

None of us were looking forward to more exploring today.

"How far are we from home?" Jahni asked.

"Not far." Joe admitted.

# 9

(Jon)

I closed my eyes and let myself fall asleep on the way home. Between the swim and the unexpected Ratillian reminder, I needed a break. Rose hummed most of the way.

"We're home." Jahni announced.

I stretched and yawned. I could see our home outside of the Com Screen. I grabbed my bag, the two boxes, and headed up the stairs. Rose was moving a little more slowly. I opened the door and set the two boxes by the door before I went upstairs to my room. I fell onto my bed and went back to sleep again. Those things called emotions were exhausting, and I was done dealing with them.

A loud knock woke me up. My eyes flew open. At first, I was surprised to find myself at home in my own bed. The door creaked open. Rose poked her head in. She saw me sitting up and closed the door behind her and rushed in.

"Jon, I'm so…" She climbed into bed with me.

"Yep." I agreed.

"Dad's on his way home." Rose covered up with my blanket.

I nodded. I looked at my WC before I remembered I forgot to charge it again. I leaned over and pulled out Rose's wrist from the blanket and looked at her Com. I had been asleep for five hours. Seriously, how did that happen? I shrugged and leaned against the wall and closed my eyes again.

"Did you look in the boxes?" Rose asked.

"No." I answered.

"Why'd you bring them?" Rose questioned.

[It seemed wrong to leave them.] I replied.

"I know what you mean." Rose was quiet for a moment. [Do you ever think about it?]

[What?] I didn't budge.

[When we lived with the Ratillians.] I could feel Rose staring at me.

"Sometimes." I told her.

"Me too." Rose was thoughtful.

More quiet. Finally, I opened my eyes. Rose was staring into space.

"You okay?" I asked.

"Yeah, just thinking too much." Rose sighed. "You really are a good brother, you know?"

I chuckled. "Okay. You're welcome I guess."

74

"And I'm a good sister, right?" Rose smiled sweetly at me.

"Yeah." I grinned.

[Dad's here.] Jahni thought to us.

[On our way.] Rose responded.

I climbed out of bed. I walked over to the closet and pulled a shirt off a hanger. Rose opened the door, and we walked down the stairs. I was finishing putting on my shirt as I reached the ground floor.

Dad hugged us both. There was no other way to say it. My father was a hugger. I rubbed my eyes and yawned.

"Hi Dad." I yawned again.

Dad examined us. "You look fine. Jahni told me about your last excursion."

"Yep." I scrunched my mouth together and moved it to the side of my jaw. [Good times. Good times.]

"We found treasure." Rose inserted.

"What kind of treasure?" Dad asked.

I walked over to the front door and picked up the two boxes and brought them to the kitchen table. Dad examined the outside of the boxes carefully. I hadn't.

He tapped the top of the container. "Joe, you said this was sixty years old?"

"Yes, sir." Joe answered.

"These are your grandfather's initials." Dad told us.

I looked at the box closer. Dad was right. I didn't have a good feeling.

"The one you were named after; Jonathan, my father.." Dad looked at Jahni and me.

"Should we contact G-Lil?" Jahni asked. "Wouldn't she want to know?"

"Take it from me, let this one go…for now." Dad told us.

Jahni gave Dad a look that said she would be talking to him later in private. I sensed her talking to him, but I didn't want to have anything to do with the Ratillians, so I was content to pretend nothing had happened.

"Open them." Rose's tone was indisputable.

Dad looked at her. He didn't say a word. Dad usually let us have what we wanted, probably because we didn't usually ask for anything absurd.

Dad left the room and came back with a crowbar, flathead screwdriver, and a hammer. He stuck the screwdriver into the crack and held the box still. The box moved slightly. Joe crossed the distance and held the box still. Dad hit the back of the screwdriver two times. He moved the screwdriver to the middle and hit the screwdriver two more times. He moved the screwdriver to the other end of the box and hit the screwdriver two times before he picked up the crowbar. He put the crowbar in the crack and hit it twice on the end and then moved it to the other end, where he hit it two more times. Dad pushed the crowbar down like a lever and pulled the box open.

I couldn't help myself from moving forward to see what was inside. It had several personal effects. Dad pulled out a jacket and placed it on the table. His hand went for an old-fashioned Com the size of my hand. It was inside a silver casing. Dad put it down. He pulled out a warped notebook. He flipped through the pages. Every page was filled in by hand from top to bottom. He laid it on top of the jacket. Three pages stuck to the bottom of the crate. He tried to lift out the paper, but they cracked.

[It's not worth it.] Dad put everything back inside the crate and opened the second.

The second crate was full of emeralds, sapphires, rubies, and pearls. Most of them were on necklaces. A few were loose at the bottom of the crate.

"Oh, my!" Jahni exclaimed.

"Where did Grandfather get these?" I asked.

"I don't know." Dad answered.

Rose bit her lower lip. She didn't say much about the topic. Salaranda walked into the room.

"Oh good, you are awake." Salaranda clapped her hands together. "Get those dusty boxes off of my table."

"Yes, ma'am." Dad answered with a smile.

After the boxes were put away, we didn't talk about them again.  Some things were hard to talk about and in this case, none of us wanted to discuss what we found and what it meant.  At some point we would, if we had to.

# 10

(Jahni)

"Where are we going this time?" Rose asked.

"Taniel." Sloane answered.

"Any particular reason?" Jon asked.

"No." I laughed.

Sloane and I had plotted out our journey according to three things: breathable air, when we needed to fuel up, when we needed to head home. Taniel fit the criteria.

"Okay." Rose began humming.

Sloane landed the Vaktow in a yellow field. We all climbed out. I couldn't see any houses or beings. There was a field as far as the eye could see. Not too far from where we stood, I saw a yellow reptile hop. It was about six inches in diameter. A big red tongue flew out and captured a bug.

"Cool." Jon commented.

Another yellow reptile hopped beside the first one. They both looked at each other and hopped away. The wind blew through and bent the wheat. It was fairly quiet.

"What's that?" Rose stuck her hand in the air and pointed to the horizon.

She was pointing at the only elevated area in sight. It looked like a large hill from where I was standing. In reality, it had to be close to a mini mountain.

"It's pretty far away. It has to be more than a hill. I bet it would be fun to climb. Want to race?" Jon suggested.

Sloane's eyes lit up. "If we are racing, I win."

"Joe, that would be cheating." Rose referred to his ability to pop to where he wanted to go in a blink of an eye, as long as it was in his line of vision.

"Fine. Coming?" Sloane held out a hand toward me and an arm to the twins.

I took Sloane's hand. Jon and Rose touched Sloane's forearm. We were at the foot of the landmass. It was no hill; it was much larger in size.

"This looks fun." Jon grinned.

"Let's start climbing from up there." I suggested, and pointed to a flat area halfway up.

"We can do that." Sloane agreed.

I blinked, and we were standing on the spot I had indicated. I looked down over the ledge and then across the field. It was a vast, open area.

"Wow!" Rose exclaimed. "We will be able to find the Vaktow, right?"

I looked in the general direction we had come from. I could barely see a speck of where the Vaktow should have been. Sloane is pretty good at finding his way around.

Jon tapped his WC. "Not a problem. I charged it this time. Joe synched our Com's to the Vaktow before we left. There is a homing beacon on it."

"Sweet! Let's go explore." Rose took off running.

Jon caught up and passed her in seconds. Sloane chuckled. I rolled my eyes.

"Help me catch up?" I asked my husband.

"Sure." Sloane grinned.

We were a few feet in front of them. Both of us took off running. Sloane laughed.

"Cheaters!" Rose called.

"Just using my resources, sis!" I shouted over my shoulder.

We ran until I was out of breath. Jon passed me, laughing. Rose almost skipped by with a grin on her lips. Sloane slowed down.

"Done already?" Jon asked.

Sloane looked at me. Jon rolled his eyes. Rose laughed. I walked over to them.

"I told you, you need to run with us. You're getting old and out of shape." Jon smirked.

"Thanks." I finally had my breath.

"Yeah Jahni. Everyone should be able to run for at least five minutes." Rose chimed.

"You're both great for my ego." I told them.

Rose and Jon laughed. Sloane grinned and slid his arm around my waist. He leaned his chin on the top of my head.

[I still love you.] Sloane thought to me.

[I'm glad someone does.] I responded.

I felt his body vibrate in a soft laugh. Jon pulled his backpack off and pulled out a water bottle. Rose took it from his hands and got the second drink. Rose handed it to me. I took a drink and handed it to Sloane. He took a drink and handed it back to Jon. Jon finished it off and put it back in his backpack.

"Where to next?" Jon asked.

"I don't care." I looked at Sloane, who shrugged.

"This way." Jon pointed.

I nodded. "Works for me."

It was mostly a bunch of trees. We were only walking for a few minutes when we found a path. It looked well-traveled.

"Wonder where it goes?" Jon was curious.

"Let's find out." Rose encouraged cheerfully.

"Which way?" Sloane asked.

"That way!" Rose pointed to the right.

I laughed. "That way it is."

The trail widened the longer we walked. The path ran into a dirt road. No one was in sight. I looked at my Com.

[Yes, people live here.] Sloane thought to me, before I had time to check my Com.

[Where are they?] I asked.

Sloane shrugged. [Not sure. Where is your sense of adventure?]

[Napping.] I grinned.

Sloane shook his head. He led the way onto the road. He looked in both directions. One was going downward, and the other was further up the mountain. We headed up the mountain.

"I would build a house up there." Sloane pointed up.

"Makes sense." Jon agreed.

"Good view." Rose agreed. "You can see someone coming from up there."

The road sloped upward until we couldn't see over it. I heard rocks being kicked against the dirt. I looked up in time to see two children run past us. They both laughed and looked at us as they passed. The boy's hair was down to mid back in five or so braids. The girl that followed him had her hair buzzed. Each of them looked over their shoulder until they were out of sight.

"Where did they come from?" Jon asked.

"I don't know." I said.

"There must be a village nearby." Rose said.

"Or at least a few people somewhere." Sloane said.

"Hey, maybe they have treehouses." Jon joked.

I looked up. I didn't see any evidence of treehouses. Rose was looking up at the trees too. She looked at me and giggled.

"Maybe not." Rose said.

We followed the road for a few minutes when we heard something creaking. The four of us stopped and looked in every direction. We heard the same noise. It was coming from high up. I craned my neck to see where it was coming from. A large limb bounced from limb to limb. We had just enough time to jump out of the limb's way as it hit the ground.

[What was that?] Jon looked around.

Suddenly, a vine swung across our path. A girl jumped off and twisted to face us. Her hair was spiked. She paced in front of us. Her smile was too welcoming.

"Who do we have here?" Her words were in the language of Zelle.

[How can she speak our language?] Rose asked.

[Her question wasn't for us.] Sloane scanned the area.

The area around us quietly filled with children of various sizes. A few of them tapped clubs in their hands. Jon readjusted his body to protect Rose, if it came to that.

[Where are the adults?]  I asked Sloane.

[I don't know.]  Sloane was ready to bolt.

"What should we do with our guests?"  The girl was obviously the one in charge.

"Throw them off a cliff!"  A small boy shouted.

"Swing them from the trees!"  A little girl yelled.

"Practice on them."  An older boy patted the club in his hand as if he was going to hit us.

"All great ideas."  The leader put a hand to her chin and scratched it.

[I think we should get out of here.]  Sloane thought to us.

[You think?]  Jon responded.

In a blink of an eye, we were gone.  We could still hear the children.  I let out the breath I had been unwittingly been holding.

"Get them!"  Their leader yelled.

"Where did they go?"  Yelled one of the children.

"Find them!  Find them!"  The children chanted.

[Let's go that way.]  Rose pointed to her suggestion.

[I don't think that's such a great idea.]  Jon thought.

The leaves started rustling behind us.  The four of us turned around and looked.  No one came through them yet.

[Okay, it's a great idea.]  Jon changed his mind.

We took off in a sprint.  We pushed limbs out of the way

as we ran. Rose was in front of me. She pushed a large branch out of the way; it came back in time to hit me in the face.

[Sorry.] Rose thought

[Let's just make a break for it.] I countered.

[Okay.] Rose agreed.

We finally found a path. A bridge was up ahead. We made it to the bridge without our pursuers in sight. By the time we heard the creak, it was too late for Jon. I looked around in enough time to see Jon fall. The three of us rushed over to the hole. He looked up at us in a daze.

"Jon, are you okay?" I asked.

He gathered himself and stood up. He started to climb up. Several bushes moved, and the leader came out, followed by her crew.

"Stay down there!" She yelled.

[You better listen.] Sloane told Jon.

Jon carefully set his feet on the ground. [How many are there?]

[They are still coming.] Rose told him.

The leader looked down at Jon. "Stay down there!"

"I will." Jon took a seat.

The leader turned around and faced the crowd. "We have caught the tall people with the funny clothes!

"We caught them! We caught them!" They chanted.

[This could be a bigger problem than we thought.]  I was concerned.

[I can get us out.]  Sloane reassured me.

[Okay.]  I had faith in him.  [Let's see what happens first.]

# 11

(Jon)

"I think this is the story of our life, Rose." I said.

We were being held in a hole dug into the side of the hill with a loose door frame. The cracks in the door was the only light available to us. I dug my shoe into the floor. The loose dirt came up in a mound. I dug my back heel into the dirt and spelled Jon and crossed it out.

"What do you mean Jon?" She asked.

"Seriously, how many times have we been captured?" I kicked a pile of dirt against the wall.

"Is that necessary?" Joe asked.

"Yeah!" I yelled, purposely sounding dramatic.

Joe grinned. "Really!"

[I don't know. Joe is with us, so it's not like we're really captured.] Rose shrugged.

She had a point. Joe would get us out of here. He had a knack for that.

"We didn't get captured on Wayr." Rose offered.

"No, just chased down by a fury beast." I scoffed.

"Point taken." Rose's nose crinkled. "I wonder where their parents are."

"Who cares?" I told her.

"Well, there has to be a reason why they are out here all by themselves." Rose told me.

"They ran away." I suggested.

"I can't imagine all of them leaving at once." Jahni told us.

[I want to see what they're capable of.] Joe told us.

"Kidnapping, beatings judging from the kid with the club, starvation, I've been hungry for almost an hour." I complained.

"We've only been on this planet for two hours." Rose reminded me.

"Still." I responded.

Rose laughed. "Don't you have any food in that backpack?"

"Some. But what if we are stuck in here longer?" I complained.

I knew the first thing for survival, food and water. I had both, for the moment. My stomach rumbled. How did people live like this?

"We won't be in here long enough to decide who's getting

eaten first." Joe grinned.

"A few hours max." Jahni agreed with Joe.

"What are you talking about in there!" Someone hit the door.

The four of us went silent. Half of the conversation had been a ploy to get them to react. Joe grinned smugly. It had been his plan.

[Good show.] Jahni winked at me.

I bowed. [If nothing else, I can talk.]

[Yeah, a bowl of hot air.] Rose grinned.

I shook my head. "Sisters." I hissed.

Jahni grinned. [Now, all we have to do is wait.]

[It shouldn't be too long. Right?] Rose asked.

"I wouldn't think so." Jahni answered.

[It's been two hours.] Joe told us.

[We're going to bail?] I asked hopefully. I was past bored a long time ago.

[If you had charged your WC last night like I said, you would have had something to play.] Rose thought to me.

[I did change it…just not all the way. Besides, this is supposed to be a vacation. Not sit around and waition.] I told her.

[Waition isn't a word.]  Rose answered.

[You knew what I meant.]  I replied.

[Yeah.]  Rose crossed her arms.

[What does it matter?  We're getting out of this pit.]  I threw the little bit of stuff I had taken out of my bag into it.

[Ready.]  Jahni stood up.

[Ditto.]  I responded.

Through the dim lighting, I could see Joe's disappearing act.  The lighting shifted as he walked through the door.  I leaned against the side of our dirt cage.

[Exactly, how long is this going to take?]  I asked Jahni.

[Not sure.  Sloane is spying on them.]  Jahni answered.

[Couldn't he have done that…oh say an hour ago?]  I asked.

[Yep, but it would have been fun explaining to these precious angels that he walked through the wall to spy on them.]  Rose answered.

[There is nothing precious about them.]  I grumbled.

[God thinks they're precious.]  Rose offered.

[He must be seeing something I am not.]  I told her.

[Yep, possibilities.]  Rose grinned.

Joe reappeared.  [I think we can handle them.  Most of them are a lot of talk.  The worst they have ever done was tie someone up and let them sit that way overnight.]

[Even the kid with the club?] My thought was doubtful.

[He wasn't around.] Joe answered.

[Okay, let's put on a show.] I grinned.

"Ooo, what kind?" Rose giggled.

[I hope this doesn't end badly.] Jahni said.

[It'll be fine.] Joe gave her shoulders a squeeze.

"Okay." Jahni smiled.

"I think the best way is to walk into the middle of their camp." Joe revealed his plan.

"That's the plan you're going with?" I asked.

"Yeah, if your sister doesn't panic all over me." Joe grinned at my sister and Jahni rolled her eyes.

"You know I'm holding your hand the whole time." Jahni told him.

"Okay." Joe grinned.

"I think I can take 'em." Rose pounded her fist into the palm of her opposite hand ferociously.

I chuckled. "Rose, don't do that." I told her.

"What?" She asked.

"All for going?" Joe asked.

"The nice way?" I asked mischievously.

"What are you thinking?" Rose demanded.

"I can do that." Joe had already read my thoughts and

disappeared. Seconds later, Joe opened the door, grinning.

"What happened to our little friend?" Rose referred to our miniature guard.

"Jon had a good idea." Joe pointed upwards.

In the distance, I could see someone jumping up and down. He appeared to be yelling, but he was so far away that we heard nothing but the wind. I laughed.

"Bet he was surprised." I patted Joe on the back.

Even Jahni laughed.

Joe took Jahni's hand and led her to the middle of their camp. It wasn't long before we were surrounded. They were mumbling amongst themselves, wondering how we got out and why we were standing there instead of trying to escape. I pulled down on the strap of my backpack, making it more snug.

"Lanock, Lanock, Ranock is gone!" Several of the children chanted.

Finally, their leader appeared. Her face was composed while she walked from one side of us to the other, searching for an answer.

"What have you done with Ranock?" She asked.

"The guard dog?" I asked.

"Yes." She said the word like she had eaten something bitter.

"There." Joe motioned with his head.

Lanock's eyes followed in that direction. I looked, barely seeing movement. Her jaw muscle tightened visibly, but her Triz were relieved.

"How exactly did Ranock get up there?" She asked.

"Show them Sloane." Jahni grinned.

"You are horrible." Rose crossed her arms, smiling.

I chuckled. "Just fun."

"Like this." Joe disappeared.

A gasp came from the crowd. Joe was standing by Lanock. He touched her arm and they both disappeared. They both reappeared before her comrades could say the first word. Everyone took a step back, eyes widened. Lanock calmed down the crowd with a wave of her hand.

"This one….brought me back. It would have been easy for him to leave me like he did Ranock." Lanock turned and faced us.

Jahni exhaled. [Sloane, you better go get Ranock.]

[What fun is that?] I asked.

[It'll help us get to the bottom of this faster.] Jahni told me.

Joe disappeared and returned with a very frightened Ranock. I bit my lips to keep from laughing. Ranock scrambled over to Lanock. Lanock patted his back and turned to face us.

"Thank you. Ranock's return is appreciated. My brother

can't keep out of trouble for nothin'." Lanock motioned Ranock to join the others, and he did.

"Your brother." Rose was taken by surprise.

"Yes." Lanock confirmed.

"What happened to your parents?" Jahni asked.

Lanock shrugged. "One day we woke up, and they were gone."

"Some were dead." Ranock added.

"Just like that?" Rose asked.

"Yep." One of the taller boys said.

"They were." An older girl agreed.

"We don't know what happened to them." A young boy played with his hair.

"How long ago was it?" I was curious.

[We have to help them.] Jahni told us.

[I thought you might say something like that.] Joe listened to every word the children said.

[All of their parents wouldn't just disappear or die.] Rose thought to us.

[Unless someone did something to them.] I replied.

[That's awful! Those poor children.] Rose's empathy flowed.

Lanock put a finger to her chin. "Oh, it's been about a season now."

"How long is a season?" Joe asked.

"Come here." Lanock ordered three children forward. They listened to her. "Hold up your hands." They did. Lanock put hers up as well. "This many days I suppose." She dropped her hands. "Now git." She shooed them away. They scrambled back to the ranks.

"And you have no clue who took them?" Jahni asked.

"Well." Lanock drawled. "Little Hopper said he saw something the night before all the parents went missing. We looked and couldn't find nothin'."

"Could we talk to him?" Joe asked, sounding very much like a king.

Lanock's eyes lit up in amusement. She turned around. Everyone was quiet, waiting for her words.

"These tall people think they can find our parents after we have looked and looked. What do you say?" Lanock put a hand to her ear.

"Hear 'em out." A tall girl bellowed.

"All in favor?" Lanock returned.

A roar filled the trees and birds flew into the air to escape what they presumed to be an upcoming attack. The yelling stopped into a stark quiet. Lanock motioned for a little boy to come forward. His steps were quick, and he stumbled over the last one.

"Go ahead Little Hopper; tell 'em what you told us." Lanock ordered.

Little Hopper took a deep breath. "Well, Momma told me not to be up late, but I heard a loud thunk, so I woked up. I saw a big flash of light and this thing took my Momma and Papa away. I hurried after 'em, but it was too dark and they went too fast to catch 'em good." The boy's chin drooped.

"You don't know if they're still on this planet." I said.

"You mean they might not be on this planet?" One of the children asked.

[Ut oh.] Rose thought.

Joe started typing on his Com. He enlarged the picture and his fingers flew. He enlarged the screen once more.

"Here is where they are." Joe held up the screen so we could see it.

"Let me see." Lanock strolled over and examined the screen.

"Does it look familiar?" Jahni asked.

A sly smile covered Lanock's lips. She turned around and faced her posse. You could hear a rock hit the ground, because of the quiet atmosphere.

"We are going to get our Momma's and Papa's back!" Lanock threw her fist into the air.

A cheer rang through the mountain. I looked at my sisters

97

and Joe. Rose was nervous. Joe was a soldier. Jahni's chin lifted in queenly dignity. We were about to go to war.

"First order of business, what road do we take to get there?" Joe asked.

"I will show you." Lanock answered.

"We can follow a map." Rose expressed her desire to go without the young group of fiends.

[I don't think they care about maps.] I thought to Rose.

[You never know.] Rose huffed.

"I am coming with you." Lanock reiterated.

"You really don't have to do that." I told her.

"Yes, I do." Lanock crossed her arms. She was unmoving.

"It will be okay." Joe's eyes were tightly zeroing in on Lanock.

"It's almost a day's travel from here." Lanock turned around and faced the crowd. "I will be back within three days. Until that time…" She looked at her little brother, and then searched the crowd. "Anthone is in charge."

A tall boy stepped out with long black hair. It was braided in various directions and hung midway down his back.

"I will keep them safe." Anthone's chin rose higher in the air.

Lanock nodded firmly. The crowd let out a cheer of approval for Lanock's choice of choosing Anthone as their temporary leader. She turned and looked at us.

"I have to grab supplies." Lanock turned on her heels and walked to the crowd. They separated and closed when she walked past them.

"Impressive." I crossed my arms.

[Well, she has kept them alive. She must be doing something right.] Rose agreed.

[She's their queen.] Jahni had a smile on her lips.

Joe pulled Jahni aside. [I need to grab some supplies too.]

[Hurry back.] Jahni kissed him.

They walked back over to us. I tossed my bag at Joe. He caught it.

"Thanks." Joe told me.

I nodded. Joe disappeared. Jahni crossed her arms. Joe returned a few minutes later. My bag was full. It wasn't long after that, Lanock came back carrying a bag on her shoulder.

"Let's go." Her voice was an order.

[Great, another bossy woman in my life.] I complained.

[You should be so lucky.] Rose grinned.

I shook my head and mumbled. "Whatever."

"The beings were huge." Lanock told us.

"What beings?" Rose asked.

"There are so many of them, and they're so big that we haven't tried to attack them." Lanock was sullen.

"You did all you could." Jahni patted her on the back.

Lanock looked at Jahni, perplexed. Her Triz said she enjoyed the encouragement. Jahni was great at making people feel better. She definitely had the knack when it came to me.

"Have you seen your parents?" Joe asked.

Lanock shook her head no. "There were so many adults there; well...I didn't really expect to see them. The morning after their disappearance...I found my Father on the floor not moving. He never moved again. He must have put up a fight during the attack." Lanock's words revealed her proud feelings for her father.

"My mother is...well she isn't exactly the tallest. You can't find her in a crowd. My Grandfather and Grandmother were not in sight when I last approached the camp. I.....haven't seen any of my people in their camp." Lanock's normal exuberance was tainted with the memories.

"How many were in this camp?" Rose asked.

A clear visual memory was etched inside of Lanock's memory of Ratillians marching through the camp. We saw it without her knowledge. Rose gasped. Lanock gave Rose a peculiar look, but did not comment on Rose's outburst. My breath caught in my throat. I didn't expect to see them here. We were looking at the Ratillians.

"There were so many in the camp I could not count them." Lanock's face was distraught.

"We have our ways of extracting people." I told her.

"I've seen your ways." Lanock looked at Joe again.

Joe chuckled.

Finally, we closed in on the Ratillian camp. We were careful not to move too much. The price of being seen was too high.

"See what I mean. There are just so many of them." Lanock complained.

[Maybe if we could distract some of them…] I let the thought trail off.

[Like a diversion?] Rose agreed. [That would probably help things.]

[A diversion.] Jahni grinned wickedly. [We can handle a diversion.] She winked at Joe.

[You are amazing.] He leaned in and gave her a kiss. "That idea was absolutely perfect."

"What?" Lanock asked. "Nothing was said."

I grinned. It was hard to remember that just because she talked Zellian, that she wasn't actually Zellian.

"Explosion. It will only take a second to put it in place and set up the timer." Joe's voice was a breath above a whisper.

"What kind of explosion?" Lanock was curious.

"The smallest kind you'll ever see." Joe answered.

Rose giggled.

I put a finger to my lips. [Rose!]

[It was funny though.] Rose answered.

I snickered.

[It might be easier if we sideline the troops.] Joe reached into his pocket and pulled out a marble size explosive.

[Sweet!] I gave my nod of approval.

[I hate to admit it, but you're right. She has already seen you pop Ranock back to camp. If it boils down to seeing you invisible, do it.] Jahni rolled her eyes.

[They don't need to know we're telepathic and empathic.] Rose reminded.

[That's a given.] I exhaled.

[I will go set this little timer for ten minutes from now.] Joe rolled the marble size bomb between his thumb and index finger. Thorton's were very small and very explosive. They were named after their inventors.

[Perfect.] Jahni cooed.

Joe disappeared. He had already given away his secret earlier.

Lanock had been looking in a different direction. "What just happened?"

I shrugged, pretending to hear nothing. Lanock frowned. She was not finding my response acceptable. She'd just have to learn to deal with it.

[Come get the troops ready.]    Joe grabbed Jahni's hand and disappeared to the Ratillian camp.

Lanock's eyes grew when they both disappeared. It wasn't too long before Joe was standing in front of us with an older couple. They looked very confused and relieved. Joe disappeared. He kept reappearing with two people at a time.

"Momma." Lanock fought to keep her voice below a yell.

The woman took off at full speed to Lanock. Lanock rushed to her. They embraced. Joe made two trips before they let go. The woman's eyes were swollen with unshed tears.

"Where is Ranock?" Lanock's mother asked.

"He's safe." Lanock assured her. "We came to rescue you."

"If I would have known, I'd have told you not to bother. I'm so glad you did." The woman paused. "How is…"

"Papa didn't make it." Lanock answered.

"I didn't think he would, but I hoped." Lanock's mother hugged her again.

The Ratillians were still unaware of our advances. Jahni

and Joe took off again for another batch of adults. They returned and left again. Soon, there were more than a hundred adults in our small space. They were doing their best to keep quiet. Jahni and Joe returned, and this time didn't take off immediately.

[They are going to notice something is up pretty soon.] Jahni walked over to me and Rose.

Joe walked behind Jahni, taking in the atmosphere. The Triz swirling around in the space were filled with excitement and anxiety. They were worried the Ratillians would discover them. I didn't quite feel suffocated by the Triz, but it was difficult to be around so much excitement and worry at once. It felt like being slapped in the face over and over.

An explosion shook the ground.

"Did it go off too soon?" Jahni asked.

"I don't think so." Joe answered.

"What do I do?" One of the adults asked.

Everyone's eyes were on Joe. He was the man with a plan, right? At least that's the way he came across. I had the feeling he made half of them up on the spot. Whether he did or not, they worked. I could count the times they didn't on one hand.

"I don't think we need to fight." Joe said.

"Ratillians tend to regroup before they make any strategic decisions." Jahni said slowly.

"Lanock, you know the way back to your home. Take them. We can find our own way." Joe told her.

Lanock's expression froze in place. Her eyes fluttered with indecision. Her mind finally settled on following orders. She wasn't used to it, but she wanted to get her family back home.

"The same route." Lanock's eyes paused on each of my sisters, Joe, and me for a split second.

Jahni nodded in agreement.

"I'll do it." Lanock agreed.

# 12

(Jahni)

I watched the last of Lanock's group walk out of view. I felt Sloane holding my hand. I jerked to attention. My gaze met his.

[Jahni?] Sloane asked.

[I'm here, I promise.] I gave him a weak smile.

[Good, we have to get the rest of those people out.] Sloane looked at Jon and Rose. "Wait here. We need someone to keep them from…"

"Doing something stupid." Jon finished.

[Yeah, an ambush from the inside while the Ratillans are this confused would get someone killed.] Rose added.

[Like us.] Jon pointed out.

"Right." I agreed.

[Leaving in three, two, one.] Sloane and I were inside of the Ratillian camp.

A Ratillian ran straight into us. I tripped and lost Sloane's grip. I saw my feet first as I became visible. The startled Ratillian got up and swung at me. I ducked. His fist went over my head.

[Sloane. Help me…now!] I told my husband.

[I'm on it.] Sloane's answer was immediate.

I saw Sloane disappear; I heard a thud behind me, and the Ratillian was on the ground. I stepped over him.

"I didn't see you." Sloane whispered.

[Watch out!] I pointed behind him.

Sloane disappeared. He was straight up in the air. I turned on my heels. The Ratillian cried out in anguish. Sloane grabbed my hand, and we became invisible.

Another explosion went off. The screams from the Ratillians rushed in mass confusion. They were running in several different directions unsure of the source of the explosion.

"We're being attacked. We're being attacked." A Ratillian yelled frantically as he passed us.

"Grab all of the important…" The Ratillian tripped over his own feet and landed on the ground.

"Get out of here." Another Ratillian scolded the one on the ground.

The mass chaos was growing into a pandemic. Most of the Ratillians were trying to escape what they perceived to be a great battle. The chaos looked insurmountable.

[Nothing is insurmountable with God.] Sloane reminded me.

[I know.] I sighed.

[You were thinking it.] Sloane squeezed my hand.

[Pretty much.] I answered.

We had already cleared the first building of Lanock's people.

[I wonder how many buildings there are. We really need a map.] I thought.

[Yeah, something simple. Please walk up to this building and we will release all hostages to you.] Sloane added.

[Yeah, that would be perfect.] I agreed.

Sloane bent down to my ear. "I have a feeling that's not an option."

I sighed. [You're sure?]

[Yep.] Sloane kept walking, almost carrying me with him.

[The guards might leave.] I thought hopefully.

[I don't know. The Ratillians are unpredictable. Sometimes they stand their ground, and other times they run. I don't get it.] Sloane shrugged.

[They do like to chase though.] I thought about my past experience when we rescued Jon and Rose. They had chased us until we were out of the atmosphere.

[Sloane over there.] I pointed in the distance. The

building was being guarded by three nervous looking Ratillians.

Sloane leaned down.  "Babe, I really can't see what direction you're pointing."

I took his linked hand and pointed it in the right direction. In the blink of an eye, we disappeared and were standing beside the building, still invisible.  Sloane walked me around and observed the Ratillian guard.

[They are definitely guarding something.]  Sloane walked me through the wall.

There were a large amount of beings inside of the small barracks.  Some were huddled in the corners, shaking.  We both took a good look around.

[I don't see any guards inside.]  Sloane told me.

[I don't either.]  I agreed.

Sloane let us become visible once again.

"Come here."  I motioned all of the people towards me.

Only two came forward of their own will.  Some hid under the beds while others stood against the wall, unwilling to move.

"It's okay.  Lanock sent us."  I told them.

"Lanock?"  An older woman said.

I nodded a yes.  She came over immediately, and so did an older man.

"Tanock's Lanock?"  The man asked.

I looked at Sloane. [Did she say her Mom's name, or her Dad's name?]

[No.] Sloane answered.

"I'm unsure, but her little brother's name is Ranock." I answered them.

A sigh of relief escaped the woman's lips. "Come." She motioned to the rest of the people, and they obeyed.

"If Lanock has sent you, it is okay." The husband agreed.

"She did. Lanock is on the way back with her mother and a large group of your people." Sloane reassured him.

"Is Ranock safe as well?" The woman asked.

I nodded.

"And Tanock?" The man asked.

I bit my lower lip. Tanock was not Lanock's mother. The man winced.

"He fought to protect his family the night you were taken." Sloane said the words so I wouldn't have to explain.

The man nodded solemnly.

Sloane held out his arm. "I'm going to get you out of here. Touch my arm."

They looked at Sloane like he had lost his mind, but they did as he asked. Sloane transferred a large group into the clearing, five travelers including myself.

"What do we do?" The woman asked when we were back

in the clearing.

"Do you know the way home from here?" Sloane asked.

They looked perplexed. Two of them shook their heads. Another one winced.

"I'll tell you what, wait until I bring you back another group and then I will point you in the right direction." Sloane's voice was authoritative.

"You don't want us to fight?" The man asked us.

"Not this time. I want you to get away and go back to your families." Sloane responded.

We went back. It only took us a few seconds to get past the guards. We took another five people back to the clearing. We were back in the barracks in seconds.

[I'll stay here this time.] I told Sloane.

Sloane looked at me. His Triz were not happy. Sloane was not the kind of man to yell immediately, so I used the time allotted to explain.

[It will be easier to take more if I'm not with you each time.] I told him.

[Okay. Hide.] His eyebrows shot up. [Hide.]

I walked over and put my body against the wall.

Sloane glared. [It'll do.]

[You'll be back in a few seconds. No worries.] I made my thoughts as reassuring as I could muster.

He looked around and gauged the surroundings. Sloane walked up the wall, disappeared, and poked his head out to watch the guards.

[They're still busy.] Sloane thought to me.

[Good.] I smiled.

[Come on, let's go. You have four trips left. Hurry up. Chop, chop.] I winked at him.

[This is not a laughing matter.] Sloane's thought was a growl.

[Stop it. You're taking it too seriously.] I grinned.

Sloane had the room cleared in less than a minute. [I pointed them down the right path. They should catch up to Lanock quickly enough.]

I nodded my agreement.

[Let's go find the next one.] Sloane pulled me into the next building. We were invisible before we made it to the other side. We walked into the closest building.

Ratillians were sitting down eating food. It was loud and boisterous. They were scrambling over the tables, grabbing plates and filling their own. Drinks were being filled. They were too involved to notice anyone that was not sitting at their table.

[Sloane, let's get out of here.] I drug his hand toward the wall.

I heard his chuckle even though he tried to stay silent. It

was a good thing the room was as loud as it was or they would have heard him.

We went into the next building. It was practically empty. There were a few boxes sitting in the corners, but that was about it.

[We can't just wander around here and hope we get everyone out.] I thought.

[We can't exactly ask the next Ratillian we see.] Sloane returned.

[Why not?] I looked at him and grinned, hoping he would agree with me.

[I can't see you smile Jahni, we are still invisible.] Sloane told me.

[Okay.] I giggled.

[Now how is this idea of yours supposed to work?] Sloane asked.

[Just go up to someone and make them think they are talking to another Ratillian. It's not that hard.] I thought to him.

[You, my lady, are a mastermind.] Sloane grinned.

He wrapped his arms around my waist and pulled me closer. The next thing I knew, his lips were on mine. I kissed him back. It wasn't too long before he lost his concentration and we became visible.

I giggled. [Did you forget something?]

He grinned. "Shut up."

He walked me to the side of the wall. He paused for a moment.

"At least I married a genius." He leaned in and kissed me again.

"One that isn't allowed to talk, apparently." I gave him a wry smile.

"You knew what I meant." Sloane retorted.

I gave him a push towards the door. [Go make it happen.]

[Okay, watch me work.] Sloane grabbed my hand and pulled me to the door.

We opened the actual door and walked through it and closed it. A Ratillian was by the door. He looked at us and saw nothing out of the ordinary. To him, we were a couple of Ratillians trying to get away from the explosions.

"Do you have a spare map?" Sloane asked.

"Yeah, you can have mine." He opened his side pocket on his pants and pulled out a folded up map. He handed the map over. "Be careful. We are still trying to find out where the attack is coming from." The Ratillian ran off.

[Told you.] I thought to Sloane.

[It worked.] Sloane grinned and leaned in to kiss me.

Sloane let the perception slip. I felt someone grab the back of the neck of my shirt. I turned around in just enough time to see Sloane's fist meet the Ratillian's face.

"Alright?" Sloane asked.

"Thanks Honey." I grinned.

"Not a problem." Sloane grinned back.

He took my hand, and he pulled me away from the mess. We looked at the map. There was one last building for prisoners. It was on the next street. Sloane popped us over immediately. There wasn't a guard. They must have scattered with the explosions. Sloane and I walked through the door.

[Who are you?] An older man stood his ground as the other shrunk away in terror. He was unaware we could hear his thoughts.

No one approached us. They huddled closer to the walls and under the beds the longer we were there.

"We came to take you back to your families." I told them gently.

"We'll be killed if we leave." The man told us.

"Yeah, the Ratillians will find us." A woman shrank into the crowd as soon as the words left her mouth.

"Bombs are going off." A man from the opposite wall reminded us.

"Safer here." Another mumbled.

"We are the ones setting off the explosions. You are safe." I tried to soothe their fears.

"You?" Another gasped.

"Why?" An older woman asked.

"As a diversion." Sloane said.

"How do you plan on getting us out?" The man in front of us spoke up.

"I can show you." Sloane offered.

"Show me then." He bravely walked towards Sloane.

[I'll stay.] I told Sloane.

Sloane's lips went into a thin line, but he nodded his agreement anyway before taking him back to the clearing. The group was stunned into silence with Sloane and the man's disappearance. I smiled nervously, unsure of their reaction. Sloane returned with the man.

"It's true!" He told them.

Cautiously, they came out of hiding and Sloane was able to transport all of them to the clearing in only a few trips.

"I think we got everybody." I told him.

"I think so too. I don't see any more prison areas on the map." Sloane agreed.

"Let's arrange a reason for the Ratillians not to come back." Sloane grinned wickedly.

"Whatcha got in mind." I was more mischievous with my reply.

"You are ridiculous." Sloane pulled me close.

"That's why you love me." I wrapped my arms around him.

"Only part of the reason." He winked.

"And the other?" I asked.

Sloane's eyes lit up, and he kissed me until I forgot to breathe. He pulled back and grinned. I let go of his waist. He freely gave his hand.

"First of all, let's take all of their food." Sloane said.

"Okay, I'm with you." I nodded my head.

"Then we need to take out all of their ammunition." Sloane added.

"Good plan." I told him.

Some ships were already scattering into the air.

"That's a good sign." I pointed.

"Not good enough. Let's get on this." Sloane pulled out a Thorton.

"You came prepared." My eyes widened and the small explosive. It was named after the couple that invented it.

"Yes, I did." Sloane's Triz were very proud.

"You had all of those in the Vaktow?" I asked.

"Absolutely." He grinned.

"I am never making fun of you for being over prepared again." I told him.

"That's my lady." Sloane told me. "You know I'm going

to hold you to that, right?"

"Probably." I laughed. "That's okay."

They had one building to eat in and one designated for food storage. Two were labeled food. We hopped off to the next place on the map. We were in the room the Ratillians had been eating in. It had cleared out from earlier. It couldn't have anything to do with the mysterious explosions, could it?

"Is anyone in here?" Sloane was met with silence. He attached a Thorton to the wall and set the detonation time. "It's their own fault for not saying anything."

"Whatever you say, Babe." I watched his attractive body work.

"Jahni!" Sloane growled.

"What?" I asked.

"I can't concentrate when you're thinking like that!" Sloane declared.

"Just admiring God's handy work." I folded my arms and continued watching.

"Let's get out of here." Sloane captured my hand.

He had me walking through the nearest wall and we were on the rooftop of a nearby building when the food building exploded.

"Let's go to food storage next, right?" I asked.

"Actually ammunition is closer." Sloane told me.

"Okay." I agreed.

The next thing I knew, we were on the rooftop of the next building. Sloane looked at the map and then he looked around. We were on top of another building. He let us fall through the roof and we landed softly on the floor.

"At least this is fun." He grinned.

I shook my head. "You're pitiful."

"You like it." Sloane winked.

"Yeah, I do." I giggled.

[Someone is in here. I can feel their Triz.] I told him.

[Maybe we should tell them to leave. If they don't listen...well that's their problem.] Sloane grinned.

I shook my head. He was impossible, and deep down, I agreed. What does that make me?

"Hey, we're going to blow up the building!" Sloane yelled.

The door flew open and several Ratillians flew out the door.

"If you want to live, you better leave!" Sloane gave one last warning.

A straggling Ratillian exited the building.

"Do you think that's enough warning?" He asked.

"I would think so." I answered.

Sloane let go of my hand and we were visible again. We

walked to the back.  There were several guns sitting on top of large crates.

"All clear." Sloane announced.

Sloane attached a Thorton to the wall and set it for 15 seconds from now.

"Sloane?" I demanded.

"We're running out of time." He took my hand and triggered the countdown.  We were out of the building within the next second.

"Food building?" I asked.

"It's right there." Sloane held up a hand and pointed to another building.

The large explosion we had just initiated caught my attention.  The fire whooshed upward and went straight down.

"It's like fireworks." I said.

"Yeah, it's fun." Sloane gazed into my eyes.  "We should do this more often.

"Really?" I giggled.

"It's a good relationship building experience, right?" Sloane put it over the top.

"Sure." I agreed.

"Too many buildings to take down before the head Rat leaves." Sloane grimaced.

I giggled. "Where is he at?"

Sloane's eyes lit up with the excitement of a plan. He looked at the map.

"Right here." Sloane pointed to the middle of the map.

Sloane looked down over the small dirt roads. We disappeared into the heart of the Ratillian camp. We were overlooking what appeared to be the base. Several Ratillians flew into the building and flew out. Some were carrying boxes of papers, and others held single documents. There was a ship a few yards from the building. Most of the Ratillians were carrying the papers into it.

[That's not good.] Sloane thought.

[We could always separate them from their precious leader.] I suggested.

[Getting brave, aren't we?] Sloane loved my plan.

[Whatever it takes, right?] I asked.

[Wait here.] Sloane motioned me not to move.

[Where am I going to go?] I asked.

Sloane shrugged and disappeared. A dressed up Ratillian stood beside us. Sloane was pleased with his ability and the Ratillian was startled.

"What in the worlds are you doing?" The Ratillian

demanded.

"Are you in charge?" Sloane asked.

"No. Why would you ask such u…" The Ratillian sputtered.

"Sorry for the inconvenience." Sloane apologized and took him back without warning.

Sloane was standing beside me again in the next second with a different Ratillian. This one seemed a bit more dignified and appalled by Sloane's touch.

"Are you in charge?" Sloane asked.

"It is none of your business." The Ratillian huffed.

"That's a yes." Sloane told me confidently.

The Ratillian's face became angry.

"What's your name and rank?" Sloane asked.

"I don't see what business it is of yours." The Ratillian retorted.

"Sargent Ganith Bore." Sloane nodded his head as if he was thinking about the name and it agreed with him.

The Ratillian's eyes pulled together in a glare. "You must have heard it somewhere."

"Not at all. I heard it from you." Sloane clearly had control of the conversation.

"I said nothing of the sort." He threw back.

"Yeah, you did." Sloane tapped his temple.

"Zellian!" Sargent Ganith Bore cried out.

Sloane grinned. "I think you finally have the right picture."

Sargent Ganith Bore crossed his arms. "I will tell you nothing more."

"Why are you here bothering these people?" Sloane demanded.

"I will tell you nothing." He spit in Sloane's direction and missed.

[I wasn't sure how he managed to miss such a close target.] I thought carelessly.

"I'm glad you did." Sloane looked at me.

The Ratillian followed Sloane's eyes until his eyes landed on me. His eyes pushed together.

"You look familiar." He looked at me.

Sloane shrugged. "I must have one of those faces."

"No, it's more than that. I can't place my finger on it." Sargent Ganith Bore complained.

"How long were you planning on staying here?" I asked.

His thought said he had come to mine for special minerals. They were planning on having the adults mine for them, but their original discovery was ill-founded. They would have left within the month anyway.

"What were you going to do with the people when you

left?" Sloane asked.

"I never said we planned on leaving." Sargent Ganith Bore retorted.

Sloane tapped his temple with his finger again.

"Curses Zellian." Sargent Ganith Bore glared.

His thought revealed he was going to kill them all. Sloane's eyes widened.

Sargent Ganith Bore saw Sloane's reaction. "I suppose you read that thought as well."

"I see why they placed you in your position. Your tact is uncanny." Sloane rolled his eyes.

"Maybe we should just come back and destroy them all." The Ratillian tossed out the bait and looked at me and Sloane to see if he had caught anything.

"What good would that do? We don't live on this planet." I told him.

"You can't possibly be going back to Zelle." Sargent Ganith Bore's voice was disgusted with the thought. "We would have detected one of your ships." The Ratillian was starting to look pale, because of his distraught nerves.

[So the Vaktow is undetectable to them.] I thought to my husband.

[That is good to know.] Sloane grinned.

"What are you two talking about? I have heard about you

people. I know what you are capable of." Sargent Ganith Bore sputtered.

"Nothing of consequence." Sloane told him in a dignified voice.

I allowed my regalness to shine in my posture.

"I know who you remind me of. You are the King and Queen of Zelle." He challenged.

"We don't have a queen or king over my planet." I told him.

His Triz told me of his unbelief.

"We have many." I said with a smile.

"I hope that you know this means war when you kill me. I will be a martyr to the Ratillian war against the Zellian creatures." Ganith Bore was haughty.

"Why would we kill you?" I grinned viciously.

Ganith Bore blanched. "What do you plan to do with me then?"

"I think we are done with him." Sloane crossed his arms. "Unless he has something to add."

"You're just going to let me go?" Ganith Bore asked in disbelief.

"You see my wife, that's her." Sloane pointed at me. "She doesn't like me to get blood on my hands and she is here right now. Count your good fortune."

Ganith Bore looked at me speculatively. He had the small amount of wisdom to keep his mouth shut.

"It's probably a good thing for you that she is here." Sloane's tone and body posture were sending a clear message of 'do not mess with me'. If I wasn't on his side, I would be scared.

Sloane took him back.

"So they don't plan on coming back. I think we just caused a minor tiff with our enemies." Sloane held up his thumb and closest finger.

"Did you just say tiff? Sloane, I think you have been having too many snacks in the kitchen. Salaranda is the only other person I can think of that says tiff." I complained.

Sloane wrapped his arms around me. "I don't know what you speak of." Sloane played dumb.

"I bet Jon and Rose are wondering where we are." I said.

Sloane kissed me and made it count before we disappeared back to the clearing.

"What took you so long? I was about to send out the search party." Rose grumbled.

"She means her. I held her at bay. You're welcome." Jon grinned.

Rose glowered at Jon. "Why did we bring you with us?"

"Comic relief." Jon shrugged.

"You need to work on your comedy routine." Rose threw

back.

Jon shrugged again. "Bad guys dead?"

"Nah, your sister thought we should let them go." Sloane answered.

"She does that." Jon answered.

"But what can you do?" Sloane shrugged.

"Can we leave now?" Rose asked.

"Let's wait until all of the Ratillians clear out." I answered.

I noticed Ganith Bore was among the first to leave. It took fifteen hours before the whole place was evacuated.

# 13

(Jon)

Lanock ran to meet us. Several adults were leaving with their children. Others were waiting around. They didn't want to go back to their secluded homes yet. Some faces were freshly washed, and others were as dirty as ever.

"Those horrid beasts did not capture you!" Lanock was thoroughly excited for the first time since I met her.

"Of course not." Rose smiled.

"Couldn't touch us." I chimed in.

"They are gone." Jahni grinned.

"For good?" Lanock asked.

"I don't know." Joe said.

Lanock's expression sobered.

"They didn't look too happy to see us. I doubt they'll be back." Joe added.

[They might come pay us a special visit though.] I told Rose.

[I hope not.] Rose replied.

[I can't believe they figured out we were from Zelle.] Jahni thought to us.

[I know, I didn't think they were that smart.] Joe finished.

Rose giggled. Lanock looked at her peculiarly. Rose threw her arms around Lanock to cover up her laugh.

"I'm so glad you have your Mom back with you." Rose told her.

Lanock was shocked, and then smiled and hugged Rose back. "Me too." There was a long pause. "Thank you."

"You're welcome." Rose grinned.

Lanock's mother walked up behind her. She had an arm around Ranock and put her free arm around Lanock. "I can't thank you enough. I only wish Tanock was here to thank you." Lanock's mother wiped her eyes. "He would have been so proud of you, Lanock; you kept everyone safe while we were gone."

Lanock smiled. "I tried Momma."

In this setting, wrapped around her mother's arm, she seemed young and sweet. She was not the young warrior that was a force to be reckoned with. Lanock's mother gave her a squeeze around the shoulder.

"I'm glad we could help." Joe told her.

Lanock nodded her agreement. "Thank you."

I looked down from the Vaktow to see all of the children waving at us.  Their parents stood behind them like protectors.  I couldn't believe it had ended that well.

Rose bumped her elbow into my side lightly.  I looked at her smiling face.  She pointed at the screen.

[That's because of us.]  Rose collapsed into my side.

I brought my arm around her.  "Yep."  I agreed.

# 14

(Jahni)

"Where to next, Joe?" Jon asked.

"It's been three days. We better head back to Zelle." Sloane responded.

"Oh." Rose looked thoughtful.

"What is it?" I asked.

"I didn't realize we had been gone that long. It only felt like a day and a half." Rose told us.

I chuckled. "I'm glad you're having fun."

"Oh, we are." Rose spoke for Jon too.

"Really?" Sloane turned around.

Jon shrugged. "I guess."

"That means yes." Rose grinned.

Jon rolled his eyes. "Whatever."

His Triz were happy, revealing Rose was right. He was enjoying the trip. I was too, except for the last little mishap. I can't believe we had to run away from a bunch of children.

"How long until we're home?" Jon asked.

"A few hours." Sloane answered.

"Good. I'm getting hungry." Jon said.

"We won't be home that soon." I told him.

Jon grunted. He peered out the screen in front of us. I yawned.

[Bout to pass out?] Sloane asked.

[I don't know what you're talking about.] "Maybe." I grinned.

Sloane laughed. "I see a pattern."

[Good night.] It wasn't long before I started drifting to sleep.

# 15

(Jahni)

[Hey, I see home.] Jon thought.

[He sounded happy.] I told Sloane.

[He is.] Sloane thought back. [He wouldn't admit it though.]

[I know.] I agreed.

We were heading straight for Zelle. Dad knew we were on our way back. The Vaktow landed and Dad was there to greet us. He looked a little relieved.

"How is everyone doing?" Dad's eyes searched over each of us taking an inventory.

"Just great." Jon said.

"Nothing we can't handle." Rose chirped.

"What's that supposed to mean?" Dad questioned.

"We had a little trouble in the bush." Sloane told him.

"Again." Dad said.

"I'm hungry." Jon complained.

"Food should be ready in about thirty minutes." Dad told us.

"Good. It looks like the planet held up okay while we were gone." Jon commented as we headed toward the door.

Dad chuckled. "You can say that."

# 16

(Jahni)

"I want to do something fun this time." Jon told us.

"You mean getting caught by little kids who want to throttle us is not your idea of fun." Rose giggled.

"Mmm not exactly." Jon smirked.

[I have the perfect planet.] Sloane thought.

[You mean the one with all of the rides?] I asked.

"Mmhm." Sloane confirmed.

"What?" Rose asked.

"We were talking about going to a planet covered in carnival rides." I explained.

"Seriously?" Jon leaned forward in his seat.

"Yes." I answered.

"Roller Coasters?" Jon asked.

"Roller Coasters and games, not to mention food stands." I told him.

"That's what I'm talking about." Jon sat back in his seat in perfect tranquility.

When we entered the atmosphere, we saw various ships flying across the sky with large banners advertising various foods, rides, and hotels. Hot air balloons lifted into the sky, carrying people. The Roller Coasters were enormous. They twisted and curved in various directions, with loops going every which way. My stomach clenched just thinking about it. I am not remotely scared of heights, but the longer I looked up, the more reluctant I became.

[Why did I say we could come here?] I asked Sloane.

[Come on Jahni. You can do it.] Sloane encouraged me.

I groaned. I wanted to retreat into the Vaktow and find some other planet. This was definitely not my idea of fun.

"What's wrong Jahni?" Rose asked.

"Nothing." I told her.

Rule one, when you're scared, don't show it. When it came down to it, the fear would take a back burner and eventually fade into something I might do again. I looked up at the coaster in front of me. Or not do again.

"I want to ride the biggest one they have." Rose declared loudly.

[That makes one of us.] I thought to Sloane.

He chuckled. [You will do just fine.]

[Why am I having a hard time believing you?] I thought

back.

"Jahni, are you coming?" Jon had taken about five steps and turned around.

I hadn't realized I had frozen in place. I told my feet to move. I walked toward Jon.

"Yeah, I'm coming." I exhaled.

"Good." Rose smiled.

I closed my eyes tightly and opened them. "Maybe we should wait to ride the biggest Roller Coaster last."

"Why?" Rose tilted her head.

"Jahni wants to wimp out on us." Jon grinned.

"Is that true?" Rose asked in concern.

[I'm still debating.] I pasted on a smile.

Rose noticed my fake smile. My sister frowned. She examined me as if she were taking inventory.

"You will be just fine. You can do it! You can do anything." Rose smiled reassuringly.

I exhaled a deep breath. "I will think about it."

"Well, think yes." Rose giggled.

I laughed with her. She was hilarious. If she only realized how close I was to turning around and hightailing it, she wouldn't be so cheerful.

"Why don't we walk around a while, before we actually get on a ride?" Sloane suggested.

"Great idea Sloane!" I agreed readily.

Rose crossed her arms and consented.

# 17

(Jahni)

"Everyone come one come all!" The subtitles jumped out at us. "Come to the amazing Hafethin Festival! You can have a chance to win a free vacation! Can you be the one to guess all of the stones in the jar?" The man's pitch was all over the place. "You could be the winner of the luxurious two day stay."

"Jahni, we got to go." Rose complained. "We haven't really done anything."

"Rose seriously, stop whining." Jon told her.

She grinned. "Hehehehe, I was pretending to be you."

"I don't sound like that." Jon complained.

"Sometimes you do." Rose laughed.

"Shut up Rose." Jon growled.

"But Jahni, can we seriously go?" She drew out her words.

"I guess." I allowed. "We have the time."

"Sweet." Jon nodded his head.

"Wait, you were asking for him." I pointed at my brother.

Rose giggled. "Yeah."

Truthfully, I was glad they hadn't mentioned the Roller Coaster in an hour. Each park entered and exited to another park. Some were themed.

"What are sisters for, if not to use them?" Jon grinned.

"You don't mean that." Rose told him.

Jon rolled his eyes. "Whatever."

There were rows and rows of booths and plenty of vendors shouting for people to come try their game. The colors were bright. The people were different from any other planet I'd seen before. It must have been popular to have half of your hair shaved and the other side long, because at least twenty people had the same hairstyle. Others who didn't have beards long in the middle and short at the sides with dramatic points.

Many people had beads and cloth woven into their hair. Outrageous colors clung to their clothes. Although, almost everyone wore black pants like a uniform.

"Where do we enter into this bogus prize?" Jon demanded.

"What do you mean bogus?" I tilted my head.

"Let's get real, a vacation for just walking in?" Jon huffed.

"You have a point." Sloane shifted his weight.

"Let's go and check it out anyway." Jon suggested.

"Just to see." I told Sloane and rolled my eyes.

Jon had his eyes on the prize. Even if I couldn't read his Triz, his purposeful walk would have given him away.

"Of course, only to see." Sloane rolled his eyes.

It didn't take long to find the right booth. The caller was yelling. Several people were writing their guesses on a piece of paper.

"Only one entry per person." The caller said.

"Great, there are four of us." Rose was overly cheerful. "That's four chances to win. We can do it!"

We all started filling out the information, except Jon. There was a large jar in front of us. It had several small round stones in it. I started to count the bottom row.

"I got this Jahni." Jon was sure of himself.

"You do?" I was doubtful.

"Jahni, watch and learn." He walked over to the caller. "Hey, sir?"

The man was startled. "What?"

"How many are in there?" Jon managed to keep a straight face.

"I can't tell you that." The caller was indignant.

"I didn't think you could." Jon walked back to us.

"Got it." [5,432 stones in the jar.] Jon was pleased with

himself.

[You cheated] Rose told him.

[I used my resources.] Jon corrected.

[Jon!] I complained.

"I want to have the prize." [Just think about how fun that would be.] Jon persuaded.

[It would be fun, but…] I wasn't convinced.

[We have what? Two more days? Three max. That is plenty of time to have this vacation and get back to Zalnorel in plenty of time to keep the ecosystem on the straight and narrow.] "Perfect plan, just sayin'." He grinned optimistically.

I wasn't so sure about that. I decided to let them 'guess' anyway. Jon was practically glowing, which was saying something. The sun even obliged and lit up his hair.

[I need you guys to guess numbers close to the right one.] Jon thought to us.

Sloane shook his head and laughed. "Okay, Jon."

"Hey, I didn't say it was just for me. You three are coming with me." Jon informed us.

Rose and Sloane jotted down the numbers. I decided to be a rebel and put down the number I was originally going to guess. It was a good three hundred and thirty-six off. I folded the paper and threw it into the jar.

"Jahni, just chill." Jon told me. "It's all about the

experience anyway." His grin was too charming for his own good.

"Jon!" I gasped.

Two hours later, it was time to announce the winner. A large crowd had gathered. We worked our way through the crowd until we were in front of the stage.

The same man was shouting. "Come one, come all! Someone has guessed the number! How astounding!"

[It was me.] Jon folded his arms smugly.

[Don't give it away!] Rose thought back.

[I'm not.] His thought was defensive.

The man made a big progression of opening the envelope. He looked even happier as he looked at the name. The crowd was silent.

"And the winner of the prize is Jon Julian. Will Jon Julian come forward?" The man announced.

Jon went to the stage. The man shook his hand and held the envelope just out of reach. The crowd laughed.

"Not so fast." The man said. "How did you pick your number?" He leaned forward expectantly.

Jon chuckled. "I'm good at math."

The crowd laughed with Jon. The man gave him the envelope. Jon bowed and walked off the stage and found us.

Jon took the tickets out of the envelope. He scanned over

the tickets. He handed them to me. They were for today through the weekend.

"Want to head that way?" Jon pointed.

I laughed. [Sounds good to me. Sloane, you ready?]

[Sure.] Sloane grinned.

"We can." I told him.

"Sweet!" Rose giggled.

# 18

(Jahni)

The driver dropped us off at the front door. Jon walked up to the desk. The attendant looked at him.

"Jon Julian." Jon said.

"Oh, the grand prize winner and his guests." The attendant said.

The being handed Jon two rings. "This will open your doors."

Jon handed one to me and slipped the other one on his finger. It enlarged to compensate for the difference in ring size. I slid on the ring Jon handed me. It shrunk to accommodate my finger.

Sloane grinned at me. "Cool trick."

I smiled. "It is."

Jon tapped the top of his ring and a number hovered three inches into the air. I did the same and saw a different number. The four of us grabbed our bags.

We walked into an open elevator. It wasn't closed off like the ones on the Jareneikian ships. It had a wide silver bar that crossed the front. The walls were a sleek silver mirror. We could see the levels move between us.

Rose grinned. "We need one of these at home."

"No, we don't." Jon rolled his eyes.

Rose skipped off the elevator. Jon slung his single bag over his shoulder. Sloane took my hand and kissed it.

Jon and Rose were in the room beside ours. Sloane and I went to our room. I needed to use the bathroom. I dropped my bag and went into the bathroom. I took a long look in the mirror before I came out. I felt like a royal mess. I leaned forward and shook out my hair. That would have to do for now.

I walked out of the bathroom. Sloane was leaning against the wall across from me. I grinned.

[I missed you.] Sloane smiled.

[I have been with you...] I thought.

Sloane took a few steps towards me and I forgot to breathe. It had been at least four days since I forgot to breathe around my husband. I thought I was getting better at this. Sloane grinned wickedly. He knew exactly what kind of effect he was having on me.

I heard a knock at the door. It was Rose and Jon. I reached to open it. Sloane stopped my hand and leaned forward and gave me a heart stopping kiss.

The knock at the door was more furious. Sloane exhaled and stepped away so I could open the door. I didn't. I stepped toward him and returned his kiss. His grin widened.

[Jahni! I know you're in there! Stop kissing Joe and open this door.] Rose complained.

I laughed and kissed Sloane again before I finally opened the door. Sloane grinned over my shoulder. Jon and Rose stood outside the door.

"It's about time." Rose complained.

"We were busy." I told her.

"I know." She rolled her eyes. "We have a lot of exploring to do. Come on!"

I tried to close the door on them. Rose stopped it with her foot. Sloane chuckled.

"I mean now." Rose complained.

"Fine." I exhaled.

Sloane took my hand in his and we followed my brother and sister. Rose trotted down the steps. Jon jumped down from the first set and landed on his feet. He jumped down from the second set and landed on his feet. Sloane popped both of us to the bottom of the stairs.

"Show off." Jon grumbled.

Sloane smirked. [Babe, was that showing off?]

[I liked it.]  I giggled.

Sloane laughed.  "Your sister's fine with it."

"Traitor."  Jon grinned at me.

# 19

(Jahni)

Jon walked out from the crowd.  He was by himself.  I scanned the crowd.

[Where is Rose?]  I asked.

"She thought she saw her friend and ran off."  Jon looked around.  "That was more than ten minutes ago."

"Have you seen Rose?"  I asked Sloane.

"Isn't she with Jon?"  Sloane asked.

"No."  I told him.

[Rose?  Where are you?]  I listened carefully and didn't hear anything.

"Rose!"  I screamed at the top of my lungs.

[Jahni, I am right here.]  Rose's soothing voice told me.

I let out a breath of relief.  [Don't you dare scare me like that again!]

Rose's laughter bounced through my mind.  [I am just talking to Anxi.]

[Where?] I needed to see her for myself.

[By the blue food cart.] Rose answered.

"Jon, where is the blue food cart?" I asked.

He shrugged. "I think I saw one over there." He pointed behind him.

I marched in that direction. Sloane was on my heels. Jon shook his head and followed us. They all thought I was overreacting. I didn't care.

I walked around a cluster of people and saw my sister. I could breathe. I stopped and so did Sloane. Jon had followed us. Sloane was smirking and Jon was grinning and shaking his head.

[I'm the Queen and if I want to be overprotective, I can be.] I told them.

Jon busted out laughing. [Now she wants to be Queen.]

[Hey, I never said I didn't want to be Queen.] I informed him.

Sloane massaged my shoulders in an attempt to calm me down. "We know."

I glared at Sloane. He backed off, both hands in the air. Jon laughed again.

Rose walked over alone. "I'm fine Jahni…See."

I looked at her. "I see."

"One of these days, you have got to stop worrying." Rose told me.

"Yeah, but not today." I smiled.

"Rides?" Sloane asked.

"I guess." I held back a full grin.

"Ooo which one first?" Rose grinned.

"How about that one?" Jon pointed at the tallest structure I had ever seen.

"No!" I exclaimed.

Sloane laughed. "Come on Jahni, with God all things are possible."

[I'm not thinking tempting God is a good idea.] I thought begrudgingly.

Sloane whispered in my ear. "Come on, I will sit beside you and hold you close. All else fails. I will have you out of there in one second flat."

I closed my eyes. He was right. I know Sloane wouldn't let anything happen to me. I opened my eyes, and he was grinning at me. He thought the whole situation was amusing.

"Fine." I glared at him.

He leaned forward and stopped a breath away from my lips. I couldn't help laughing. His grin widened, and he leaned over and kissed me. I shook my head and followed them to the most ridiculous ride on fifteen planets.

The line was longer than a standard Jareneikian ship and that was saying something. Jon leaned against the railing. Rose climbed up and sat down on the railing, and leaned on Jon's arm. Sloane wrapped his arm around me to calm me down.

Two hours later, we were at the gate. I took a deep breath in. Sloane would keep me safe.

[It will be fine.] Sloane winked.

[I know.] I admitted.

We walked onto the ride and fasted in. I clung to Sloane's fingers. He grinned. Rose was giggling and excited. Jon leisurely put his arm around the back seat of the ride. I didn't understand how they could be so calm.

The ride started with a jerk. Sloane will get me out of here if this ride fails. I am fine. I will be fine. The ride dropped ten feet. A scream bailed out of my mouth. Sloane laughed. The ride flattened out and then went in a loop. My stomach jumped into my throat.

[I am not going to throw up.] I ordered myself.

[Yeah, don't do that. I'm right in front of you.] Jon thought.

[Gee thanks for your consideration.] I told him.

[Aim for good old Joe. He won't mind.] Jon distracted me.

[Yeah, he would.] Sloane returned.

[This is the best!] Rose thought to us.

[No, it's not.] I thought as the ride went into another loop.

[Wait for it Jahni, here comes the drop.] Rose warned. Her scream went through the air as we dropped again.

[It's half over Jahni.] Sloane told me.

[Okay.] I answered.

I gritted my teeth. I didn't like the force in which the air hit me. My eyes were drying out. I tried blinking. It got worse.

We went straight up. I could see the ground below me. It was almost as if we were flying into the sky. I felt dizzy. We finally got over the hump.

[Sorry Jahni.] Jon told me.

[Sorry?] I asked.

Then I knew what he meant. I saw several spirals in a row directly below us. We plummeted into one spiral, and another, and another, and a fourth before dropping an additional several feet.

The ride finally came to a stop. The seat belts came off. I was never so thankful to set my feet on the ground. I stumbled the first few steps.

Jon laughed. "You made it, sis."

I glared at my brother. Sloane stretched. We walked out of the exit gate.

"I'm so proud of you, Jahni." Rose told me.

I grimaced. [Was I that bad?]

[Worse.] Jon answered. [Notice your husband isn't

saying a word.]  Jon laughed.

Rose giggled.  "You tried it, that's what's important."

"Wanna go again?"  Jon taunted.

"No."  I growled.  "Next time I'm watching."

Sloane chuckled.  [I'm just glad you didn't puke on us.]

[It was a close one.]  I smiled.

"Ooo gross."  Rose complained.

"It's a bodily function Rose, it happens."  Jon grinned.

Rose glared at him.  I laughed.  They were a good distraction.  It was several minutes before my stomach calmed down.

# 20

(Jahni)

[Sloane, what was I thinking?] I said.

"You were thinking you wanted to see the surrounding galaxies." Sloane replied.

"Okay, but I didn't think this would actually happen. Where do you think Jon and Rose are?" I was getting more worried than I wanted to admit. Sloane obviously saw right through me.

"Don't worry Jahni, we'll find them." Sloane reassured me.

"But what if…?" I asked.

Sloane stopped and took my hand in his. "God will help us."

"Okay." I answered.

This was the second time in one day that I had lost Rose. Jon wasn't exactly short. I should be able to find him in this mess.

*[God help us find Jon and Rose. Amen.]* Sloane prayed.

[But where do we look first, Sloane?] I asked.

[Over there.] Sloane indicated to my right.

I looked to where Sloane had indicated. Jon and Rose stood there talking to each other. We found them.

[Okay.] I breathed a sigh of relief. [Thank God.]

[Ditto.] Sloane grinned at me as if I were the cutest thing on twelve planets.

I clung to Sloane's hand. There was no way I would allow myself to get lost here. We made our way to Jon and Rose.

By the time we got there, they were gone. I looked around. I didn't see them. Sloane squeezed my hand.

[Do you think they'll be okay?] I asked.

[Yes. They just went to the bathroom.] Sloane smiled. [I saw them walk through that door.] Sloane pointed.

[I think I should go too.] I told him.

Sloane shook his head. "Fine. I will wait here."

I walked to the end of the line. It was huge. They probably just got stuck in this ridiculous line. Sloane was right.

[Jahni? Is that you?] Rose thought.

[Yes.] I was relieved.

[Were you panicking again?] Rose asked.

[Panicking is a strong word.] I thought back.

[That's a yes.] Jon thought from the other bathroom.

[Come up here. I'm towards the beginning.] Rose thought.

I didn't like to cut in line, but my paranoia took over. I got several disgruntled stares as I passed beings to the beginning of the line. I felt guilt slip around me like a deep puddle.

*[I'm sorry God. You are a merciful God. I don't need to be worried. Please watch over me, my husband, my brother, and my sister on this trip. Your protection is more than enough. Amen.]* I prayed.

*I have never failed you, have I?* God answered.

*No.* I felt like I had been reprimanded.

*Do you think I will fail you now?* God asked me.

I thought about the question before I answered. I wanted it to be honest. I did believe God would be there for me in any circumstance. We were safe in MaCownia and on many other worlds; I admitted.

*No. You won't fail me. I am sorry. I will try to let this worry slide away.* I prayed.

*It's time to work on you trusting in me.* God answered.

*Okay. I agreed.*

I didn't want to know exactly what that entailed. I found Rose. She grinned at me. I smiled back.

"See, that wasn't so bad." Rose said.

"I guess not." I tried to let God calm my nerves.

We went to the bathroom, washed our hands, and made a hasty exit. Jon was chilling beside Sloane. They both were grinning at us when we came out.

[Stop that.] I ordered.

[Oh, the Queen has spoken.] Jon chuckled.

[Stop teasing Jahni.] Rose defended me.

Jon stood up and kept laughing. Sloane tried to stop his

laughter and failed.  He was not helping things.  I gave him a mock glare.  It didn't do anything about the situation.  I gave up with a sigh.

"It's okay, Jahni."  Sloane told me, still grinning.

"Subject change please."  I pasted a fake grin on my face.

"Food."  Jon volunteered.

"I could do food."  Rose agreed.

[I can always do food.]  Sloane winked.

"Food it is."  I accepted the new distraction.

# 21

(Jahni)

I tried to move, but Sloane's grip around my waist tightened. I patted his hand in an attempt to get him to let go. The sun was brightening the room quickly. We still had a lot to see while we were on this planet. Sloane was out of it. He exhaled and his breath hit my neck.

[Sloane, it's time to wake up.] I thought to him.

He started to dream. He was back on Deltik, walking into his home with Starlin and Marta. Before he got in the door, he jumped into a Vaktow and was racing in Zalnorel. Within a few seconds, the Vaktow vanished, and he was walking into his office. Work called, and he left for an emergency meeting.

[Sloane.] I tried again.

His dream shifted to me. We were at home. I was standing on the stairs. He popped beside me.

I moved from side to side, trying to get free, but Sloane stayed asleep. I wiggled around until I was facing him.

"Sloane? Wake up." I told him.

He mumbled an unrecognizable word. I planted a kiss on his lips. He returned it. His eyes opened sleepily.

"Hey." Sloane yawned.

"Hey yourself. You had a pretty strong grip on me while you were sleeping." I told him.

"I did?" He loosened his grip. "Sorry."

I rolled my eyes. "Love you." I kissed him again and crawled out of bed.

"Love you too." Sloane stretched.

I took a shower and was dressed before Sloane made it to the bathroom. I walked to the window. It was getting late. I wonder why Jon has been pounding on the door yelling at us to get this show on the road.

"I'm going to check on Jon and Rose." I told Sloane before I left the room.

[Okay.] Sloane answered.

161

I left my room door open a crack and walked next door. I knocked on the twin's door.

[Jon!  Rose!]  No answer.

I frowned.  Jon should have answered the door by now. He wakes up early like I do, so why haven't they answered?

[Sloane!]  My thought was too loud.

Sloane was beside me instantly, shirt gaping open. [What's wrong?]

[Jon's not answering me.]  I told him.

Neither of us expected Rose to answer.  She was never awake until someone dragged her out of bed.  Sloane walked through the door and back out, holding a note.  He handed it to me.

Left early, wanted to get a head start on the rides.

Com you in a bit.

Jon

## Rose

I crumbled up the note and marched back to the room. Sloane finished getting dressed while I tried to get Jon and Rose on the Com.

"They probably can't hear their Com's over the noise." Sloane poked his head out of the bathroom.

"I'm going to kill them." I answered as I pulled on my shoes.

"Death by hug. There are worse ways to go." Sloane popped to his shoes, then popped to the bed to put them on. Sloane put out his hand, and I took it. We turned invisible, and he allowed us to fall through the floors until we made it to the first floor. Most of the occupants were asleep. A few had left earlier, leaving messed up blankets on the bed.

Sloane had us in the breakfast area in seconds. I frowned.

"I'm not leaving this hotel without eating." Sloane

marched to the buffet table. He grabbed a sandwich and put a closed drink in his front pocket. I didn't move. "Babe." His eyes narrowed.

I exhaled sharply and grabbed a piece of fruit and a bottled drink. I took a bite to show I was eating.

[Thank you.] Sloane's thought was gentle.

Part of me wanted to cry and the other part of me wanted to be mad. I swallowed both emotions, and we headed out the door.

No one paid attention to our arrival or departure from the room. We left the hotel and started searching the streets.

# 22

We walked around the corner.  The blue green creature growled.  His language was gargled.  Subtitles jumped out of his mouth.  Several beings stopped and stared as he talked.  He smiled.

[Sloane?  Did you see that?]  I couldn't see him, but knew he was hovering over my shoulder.

[Look at his shirt.]  Sloane sent a visual image of a pendant on the being's clothing.  It was about the size of my fingertip.  [It's actually quite considerate.]

[Okay, I will admit it is a little considerate.  A little creepy, but considerate.]  I thought.

[I agree completely.]  He thought back.

[He looks a little angry.]  I told him.

[That's because he is angry.] Sloane thought back.

*"You need to leave immediately or I will have to kill you and throw you in prison in that order."* The subtitles read as the beast gurgled.

[Did he just say what I think he said?] I asked Sloane.

[Yep.] Sloane confirmed.

[What sense does that make?] I asked. [He will kill us, then put us in prison. Really? Think about what you're saying.]

*"And I will eat you and then demolish your insides."* He gurgled; the subtitles read.

[I can't take this anymore!] I told Sloane.

[I know, but play it cool. He does have the upper hand.] He told me.

[I know. I know.] I admitted.

"We were just looking for her brother." Sloane told the being.

The being paused and looked at us. A less intimidating gurgle came out of his lips. *"I have seen someone like you around. He had white hair. We thought he was an intruder."*

"That's him." I said.

"He is not an intruder.  We just want to take him home and leave."  Sloane replied.

*"That way."*  The being pointed relieved we were going away.

Sloane and I walked in that general direction.  The being gurgled.  We turned around to see the subtitles.

*"Good luck finding him."*  The being gurgled a laugh. *"And if you get caught...so be it."*  The laughter was louder as he walked away.

"Well, that's reassuring."  I rolled my eyes.

[Is the stress starting to get to you?]  Sloane asked.

[No, but thanks for checking.]  I smiled.

We walked in the front door.  The lights were dimly lit, making it feel like a cavern with torches.  The brown walls absorbed the light.  Each hallway led to a series of doors, followed by another hallway.  The maze was bigger than necessary.

[Not here or there or there.]  I thought to Sloane.

I didn't bother opening the doors as I passed them.  I know Jon's Triz from this distance. If I didn't feel him, he isn't in there.  I stopped and looked at Sloane.

"I don't think he is on this floor at all."  I frowned.

"It's okay.  Do you want to go up a floor or down a floor?" Sloane asked.

I thought really hard. "Let's go down a floor."

Sloane took my hand, and we were beside the staircase we had passed a minute before. Sloane looked downstairs, and we were there. Sloane let go of my hand.

I looked around. "I don't think this is the right floor either."

"Okay. Do you want to go down another floor or back up?" Sloane asked me.

"Let's go down one more floor." I told him.

We walked downward. I listened carefully. I felt the back of my neck bristle anxiously.

[Jon!] I thought firmly.

Nothing. I couldn't shake the feeling that he was down here. I rushed down the steps. Sloane kept my pace.

[I know he is down here.] I told Sloane.

[Okay.] Sloane agreed.

We walked down the hallway. I marched past several doors until I was at the end of the hallway.

"This one." I told Sloane. "He is in here."

Sloane took my hand, and we walked through the wall. Sloane took me at my word.

[Jon, where are you?] I sensed my brother's presence.

[Right here.] Jon answered.

I ran across the room to the door and peeked through the window. I saw Jon sitting in a chair tied up. Sloane didn't wait for an invitation, before he gave me a push through the wall.

"Help!" Jon called.

Before I could move, a shadow fell over Jon, touched his back, and Jon slumped in his chair.

My jaw went slack as Jon stepped out of the shadows, grinning from ear to ear.

"You mean that was a robot?" I asked, dumbfounded.

"Well yeah. Didn't you see the rubber syntax of it? Dead giveaway." Jon said. "How could you even mistake that for a person, Jahni?"

I threw my arms around him. "Where have you been?"

"Well…It's a long story." Jon answered.

"I'd love to hear it." I told him genuinely.

"Hey where is my sister at?" Jon asked.

"Right here." I said.

"No, the other one." Jon answered.

"No idea." Sloane said.

"We've been hunting down both of you." I said.

"I think it's time we find her." Jon was stern. Not really worried, but ready.

"Okay." I said. [Maybe he has better ideas than we have.] I told Sloane.

[Or better connections.] Sloane thought back.

Sloane and I had both noticed Jon and Rose could share thoughts from longer distances than any other Zellian we have met. I personally thought it was because they were twins. Sloane thought it had to do with practice and growing up on Ratilles.

"Do you know where to look?" Sloane asked.

"Of course." Jon said proudly. "Keep in mind we have to get back to Zalnorel soon."

[No kidding?] I thought to Sloane sarcastically.

[I think your brother is rubbing off on you.] Sloane teased.

[Probably.] I admitted.

Jon touched Sloane's forearm. "Let's get out of here the quick way."

"Fine with me." Sloane agreed.

We walked through the door. A moment later, we were at the foot of the stairs. Sloane looked up, and we were at the top of the steps.

[Let's go out this way.] Sloane thought to us.

Sloane walked straight through the wall with us on either arm. We were on the ground floor. The sunlight hit our face.

"Thank God." I was more at ease.

One problem was solved. Rose was another story. Jon knew where she was; at least that's what he said.

"How did you get in there anyway?" Sloane asked.

"It was supposed to be some fun house. And trust me, it wasn't fun." Jon told us.

"Where was Rose when you went in?" I asked.

"Rose didn't want to go in. She said she would wait by the door for me." Jon explained.

"She wasn't there when you got back?" I was concerned.

"I didn't get a chance. I was ambushed, and she was too. I had made it to the second floor when four guys attacked me, they pushed me against the window in time for me to see Rose fighting off a few guys and fell to the ground, they stuck me with a needle and I woke up in that room." Jon told us.

Jon looked around. He took off across the street. We followed him. He stopped and listened carefully and darted down a back alley. He paused again and hung a right. He stopped two buildings down.

[She is in there.] Jon shook his head.

I listened for thought patterns. [Two beings are downstairs.]

Jon nodded. [Rose is one of them.]

Sloane took my hand and put his hand on the back of Jon's neck. We were invisible and walking through the wall. One of the beings was watching the screen intently and laughing. Sloane popped us to the door frame. The boards creaked under our sudden weight.

"Who's there?" The being bellowed.

We didn't move. The being looked around cautiously before he returned his attention back to the screen. He laughed loudly. Sloane popped us on the other side of the next room.

[No one else is here.] Jon stepped out of Sloane's grasp.

[Have it your way.] Sloane told him, firmly holding on to my hand.

Jon walked up to the door in front of us. [She is in here.]

The back door opened. Someone else started talking. Jon looked at his back. He had not been spotted.

[We need to be in that room now.] Jon thought.

Sloane pushed him through the wall and we walked through it. The room was empty. Jon looked around the room in confusion.

"Impossible.  I know she is here." Jon thought.

# 23

[Rose?]  Jon thought her way.

"In here."  Rose's voice came from behind a shelf.

We walked over and moved the shelf out of the way.  A locked door was hidden behind it.  Jon was right, she was here.

[These guys aren't very nice.]  She was as happy as a bird flying above the shore.  [And their Com Screen's barely work at all.]

Sloane walked us through the door.  Rose was sitting in a dimly lit room.  She was handcuffed to a chair.

Jon pointed out her attitude first.  "Rose, you're starting to sound like a spoiled…"

"Princess."  She laughed.  "I thought I would try something new."  She giggled.

"Please don't. I like you just the way you are." I told her.

"Aw. That's sweet. Now let's get out of here." She told us.

Jon pulled out a lock pick kit and opened the handcuffs in ten seconds. "Hey, that actually worked." He grinned.

"How do you get yourself into these messes?" I asked.

Rose shrugged. "Next time, I am going to choose the scary house, that's for sure."

"Good, at least you got some sense kicked into you." Jon grinned.

Rose ran to him. He picked her off the floor and twirled her around. She was all smiles.

She gave a quick group hug and pranced out the door. "Which way?" [We have a planet to save. I don't think Dad will like it if we destroy Zelle's life force again.]

[The first time we had a pretty good excuse.] Jon thought.

[Yeah, but not twice.] She grinned.

"Spending half the day locked up isn't my idea of fun." Jon grumbled under his breath.

[It's almost a day's drive home.] Sloane added.

Great, we were running out of time. We were nearing the end of the hall. Rose stopped and turned around. We stopped behind her.

[By the way, there is only one guard here. For some reason, he acts like I'm going to escape or something.] She grinned.

[You escape?] Jon asked mischievously.

[Definitely.] Rose joined him.

[Two guards. We heard one come in.] I thought to Rose.

[Come on Jahni. One guard. The buffoon on the couch hardly counts.] Rose grinned.

[Game plan?] Jon asked.

[Sloane?] I asked.

[Oh, I'm supposed to have the plan?] Sloane asked.

[Don't you always.] I countered.

[Yeah. Here is what we are going to do.] He began.

We all leaned forward. I heard someone moving in the next room. Sloane took my hand in his. Jon slid his hand on

Sloane's forearm. Rose did the same. We became invisible and walked through the nearest wall. We were in a trashed room with a bed. We walked through the next wall and were outside.

[Two rescues in the same day? This is getting ridiculous.] Jon joked.

[I agree.] I told them.

Rose looked sheepish. [Sorry Jahni.]

[It wasn't my fault.] Jon crossed his arms.

[Let's leave this planet.] Sloane said.

[K.] Jon agreed.

[Dad is not going to let you off world ever again.] I complained.

[You don't have to tell him.] Jon was walking away faster than I liked.

[I am surprised he let us come after Jon tried to make a break for it and fell asleep on the beach.] I rolled my eyes and rushed to catch up with my brother.

[I thought we decided to never talk about that again.] Jon told me.

[Nope, don't think we did.] Rose skipped beside Jon.

[That could have been bad.] I told them sternly. I don't want you ever leaving me like that again.

[Okay, Mom.] Jon exaggerated.

I felt a twinge of pain. Sloane sensed my Triz and took my hand. I tried to smile at him, but couldn't. He nodded once to let me know he understood.

Rose finally sensed my Triz and elbowed Jon in the side. [We won't do it again. Promise. Right Jon.] She threatened Jon.

I heard him exhale. [We won't leave early without you next time we are off world.]

[Thank you.] I squeezed Sloane's hand for moral support.

# 24

(Jahni)

We made it to the ship safely.

"Do we have to go home?" Rose pleaded.

Our ship was halfway to Zelle.

"You don't want to go home?" I asked.

"If we go home, Dad will ask what we did on our trip." Rose's nose scrunched up.

"Oh." I commented.

"He won't want us to finish our trip." Jon complained.

"And I don't want our adventure to end like that." Rose's eyes were wide with concern.

"And what makes you think I want to do another round?" I asked.

"Please Jahni!" Rose begged.

"Yeah, I promised." Jon added.

I exhaled sharply. [Sloane, can we just swing by Zelle, so we are close enough to start over on our time?]

[Yeah.] Sloane grinned.

[Thanks.] I smiled.

[Softy.] Sloane laughed.

"Fool, is more like it." I muttered.

"So that's a yes?" Rose asked.

"I guess so." I closed my eyes and exhaled.

"Thank you Jahni! Thank you Joe!" Rose yelled.

Jon leaned back in his seat. He crossed his arms. A slight grin lit my brother's lips.

"There is a catch." I added thoughtfully.

Sloane chuckled, because he heard my thoughts.

"What?" Jon demanded.

"You have to call Dad and tell him." I grinned at my brother.

"But…" Jon complained.

"We'll do it." Rose glared at Jon.

Jon shook his head no at Rose.

"Com, call Dad." Rose gave the command to the Com.

The screen popped up, and we saw Dad sitting at his desk.

"Hold on." Dad told us and the Com screen froze in place.

The automated greeter appeared on the screen. "The person you are trying to reach cares about your call, but is unable to communicate at this time. If you would like to watch a music video until said person is available, pick your preferred genre at the bottom of the screen." She pointed downward.

"Yes. Top 30." Rose ordered.

The number one video of the week began to play. Before the song reached the second verse, Dad answered.

"Sorry about that guys." Dad began.

"It's okay." I answered.

"How is everything?" Dad asked.

"Err…" Rose fumbled words to say.

"Fine. We won a trip and stayed in a hotel free of charge." Jon answered.

"That's cool. You on your way home?" Dad asked.

"Nah, trying to get as much in as possible." Jon grinned.

Dad's eyes narrowed. "Jon's doing all the talking."

"Sorry Dad." Rose apologized.

"For?" Dad knew something was up.

"How 'bout we tell ya when we get back?" Jon suggested.

Dad exhaled. "As long as it wasn't illegal or immoral."

"Not us." Rose hurried to contradict the statement.

"Promise Dad." Jon put on a fake smile.

Dad closed his eyes. "I don't want to know."

[No, you don't.] Rose thought loudly.

[Jahni, do I need to know something.] Dad asked.

[I'll tell you all about it when we come back.] I told him.

[Okay.]  "Love you.  Stay safe."  Dad told us.

"We will."  Rose hurried to answer.

"Ditto."  Jon told Dad.

"Want to see something cool?"  Sloane asked.

"Always."  Jon said.

"Definitely."  Rose agreed.

"We are near the planet Neik. Rumor is Hanlin is supposed to be crowned King in a few hours.  We could be party crashers."  Sloane suggested.

"Do it."  Jon told him.

"I'm in."  Rose agreed.

# 25

(Jon)

There was mumbling among the guards. One of them pointed our way.

[What are they doing?] Rose asked.

"Mmmemuh." I shrugged.

They came walking towards us with purpose. They started talking at once. Before I knew it, both of my arms had been captured and I was being held down. My backpack fell to the ground. Rose picked it up and swung it over her shoulder.

It would be easy to get out of this predicament. Their weapons hung on their belts. I could easily get out of their grasp. A kick to the right one's leg, followed by an elbow to his stomach, would be distracting enough. Then I could spin using my body weight in my favor and throw the left guy off balance, kick him in the gut, followed by a punch to the face. Before they recovered, I would be gone.

[Don't do it Jon.] Joe thought.

I let out a deep breath. [Calm down Joe, I didn't say I would do it. I just thought it would be easy.]

[Not on this planet.] Joe went into warrior mode.

[This better be good.] I complained.

[Although, they look like they are not armed, I can see four weapons pointed in your direction.] Joe told me.

[Where?] I scanned the area in front of me.

In the tallest building in front of me, I saw a gun pointing at me. I scanned the building to my right and saw another. I looked at my left and saw a third. Most likely there were three more behind me. It's a good thing I am less impulsive than Rose. I would have already had a bullet in my chest by now.

[We'll get you out.] Joe promised.

I scanned their thoughts. [They don't have anything on me. I think they were hoping for a reaction. Good thing I didn't give them one. I should be out in a few hours. Don't worry about it.]

"Where are they taking Jon?" Rose shrieked.

Jahni put her arm around Rose's shoulder. She looked concerned as I was pulled away. They threw me into a small vehicle with bars on it. They climbed into the front and drove off.

I left a clearly depicted picture of where I was going for my sister's and Joe to follow. I could wait out their accusation since I hadn't actually done anything, but I wanted a ride home when they kicked me onto the street.

The one in the passenger seat tapped his wrist and began talking into it. I couldn't make out any of his words. I wish he had one of those annoying subtitles running with his conversation that Jahni said she saw on the carnival planet. I crossed my arms and pushed my knees against the seat. The passenger turned around and looked at me, thoroughly annoyed. I smirked. He spouted off angrily in another language. I shrugged. His face turned bright red. I said nothing and looked out the window.

[We might have a problem if they figure out who you are.] Joe thought to me.

[Dad would probably appreciate it if we avoided galactical conflicts with other worlds.] I let out a deep breath.

[Probably.] Joe agreed.

Good thing I have a brother-in-law that can walk through walls, right?] I grinned.

[Right.] I could feel the amusement in Joe's Triz.

# 26

(Jahni)

[Sloane.] I looked around for him.

The crowd kept pushing from every angle. Apparently, these beings were unaware of personal space. I tried to look around the beings, but my height made it impossible.

"I'm right here Jahni. I wouldn't leave you." Sloane assured me.

"I know." I didn't feel as sure.

"We have to find Jon." Rose said.

"We will." I told Rose. [Right Sloane?] I thought to my husband.

"He is only being detained." Sloane said.

"Detained is one step away from locked up forever." Rose complained.

"Hon, Sloane can walk through walls. We can get Jon out." I put an arm around her shoulder.

We were almost at the end of our track. Jon's directions had been vivid. The building we approached was massive.

[Don't try to make me feel better, Jahni. I can't until he is out.] Rose proclaimed.

[Sweetheart.] Sloane thought.

[Ut oh…you only call me Sweetheart when something is about to go wrong.] I turned my full attention to him.

Sloane grimaced. [Guilty. The detainment center has restrictions put in place to keep people like me out. If I tried to walk through the wall, an electric current large enough to disable a Vaktow would go coursing through my veins.]

My jaw dropped. [You are not allowed to walk through walls on this planet.] The thought came out as an order, but he noted the concern behind it.

[Point taken, I will play safe.] Sloane snuck into the building through the front door as someone left.

[Joseph Smeltzer Sloane!] I yelled the thought. [You were supposed to say, of course not.] I growled the last thought, scared for his safety.

[Love you.] He thought instead.

[Sloane!] I thought back.

He was listening, but refrained from answering. His Triz weren't nervous at all. That did make me feel somewhat better.

[Come on Rose. We need to go to the 'bathroom', right? And that looks like the perfect building.] I indicated to the detainment facility.

[Yes sister, I believe I do.] Rose grinned.

[Jahni!] Sloane thought.

[Two can play at this game Babe, see you inside.] I thought back.

[Fine.] He agreed begrudgingly.

Rose and I walked right up to the door and entered. The people inside stopped as soon as we came inside. Ut oh, not a good sign. It is easier to get things done when people are avoiding you.

One of them spoke up, but it was in another language. Rose tapped her Com, and it started translating our conversation.

"Who are you?" One of them asked us.

"We are looking for the facilities." Rose told him.

"Over there." He nodded off to the left.

"Thank you." I said.

We went into the bathroom. I looked under the stalls. The room was empty except for the two of us. How were we going to escape and find Jon?

[Coast is clear.] Sloane told us.

[Thanks Babe.] I thought. [Come on, Rose.]

[Right behind you.] Rose thought.

[Through those doors.] Sloane sent a visual of the doors closest to us.

I grinned. Rose was on my heels as we disappeared through the doors. The hallway was startlingly quiet.

[Jon.] Rose thought clearly.

[What are you doing here? Get out!] Jon told us.

[We are not leaving without you.] Rose informed him unmoving in her resolve.

[You better be careful.] Jon's thought was a growl. [Why did you let them come here, Joe?]

[There is no stopping either of them.] Sloane thought.

[How did I get such opinionated sisters?] Jon complained freely.

[Just lucky I guess.] Rose grinned. [Where are you J?]

[Fourth door from your left. I counted as they led me in.] Jon thought smugly.

[I knew you had brains.] Sloane thought.

[Just get me out, before they realize who I am.] Jon told us.

[Done.] Rose told us.

I heard footsteps. We pressed ourselves against the wall. I slid my hand into Rose's. I held out my other hand. Sloane's fingers were through mine in a heartbeat. We disappeared. Two beings came into view. They didn't bother looking up as they walked past us.

We followed the beings down the hallway. They went into a room. The door closed behind them with a loud thud.

[Jon, are you in there?] Rose thought.

[What do you think?] Jon thought back.

[Good.] I exhaled the breath I had been holding.

They were in there for a long time. Finally, they came out. They walked down the hall and rounded the corner. Sloane opened the door and went in.

"Jon!" Rose threw her arms around our brother.

I breathed a sigh of relief. "Thank God."

[Love you too Rose, let's go.] Jon told her.

Sloane stuck his head out the door. [We have a problem.]

[We are not allowed to have any more problems.] I told him.

[Three beings are blocking our exit.] Sloane told us.

[Why?] Rose was upset.

[Oh, great. They are moving that weirdo now.] Jon thought.

[Who?] I frowned.

[He has three eyes and looks like a creeper. He's wanted in seven planets for murder and theft.] Jon told us. [They thought I was here to bust him out.]

[Ut oh.] I thought.

[What?] Sloane didn't like where this was going.

[If they thought Jon was going to bust him out…] I stopped.

[Then someone will.] Rose finished.

[We are about to get ambushed?] Jon asked.

[You said it.] Rose thought.

[You're right.] Sloane groaned. [The only question is here or in the middle of transport.]

[If Jon escapes now, he will be associated with this guy.] Rose told us.

[Jon, did they already take your prints?] Sloane was concerned.

[I think so.] Jon's Triz were somber. [The table lit up when I touched it.]

[We have to eradicate his information, so it won't tie him back to Zelle. This could start an all out war.] Sloane pounded his fist against the wall. [I'm sorry Jon. You have to stay, at least until we can hack into the system.]

[I'm not going anywhere.] Rose thought firmly.

[Rose, you can't stay. They will notice.] Jon tried.

[I don't care.] Rose was adamant.

[Don't be ridiculous, Rose. One Julian held in detainment is more than enough. If they find you here, they will take you away and you would still not be with me. Then we would have a bigger issue.] Jon stared her down.

[Look at this face.] Rose pointed at herself. [Does it look like I care?]

[Rose!] Jon yelled.

[Jon!] Rose matched his energy.

[Jahni, get out of here before these idiots discover my pain in the butt sister.] Jon glared at Rose.

Rose returned his glare with the biggest smile in the world. [I will wait over here.] She stepped back to the corner behind the door.

Jon crossed his arms and sat back down. [Don't touch anything.]

I looked at my fingers. They were bare. We were about to

hack into Jon's files and eradicate them. We would be touching something.

[Here.] Sloane handed me a small tube. [Rub it over your fingertips. It covers up your prints. They won't recognize our species.]

I did as he instructed. I heard an explosion.

"Crap!" Jon closed his eyes.

[I will be right back.] Sloane loosened my hand from his.

[Sloane!] I complained as he disappeared and the door opened.

[Give me a minute.] Sloane answered.

[Okay.] It wasn't as if I could stop him. He was already out the door. [Men!] I let him hear the thought.

I felt his Triz of amusement in return. I looked at my brother and sister. I tossed the fingerprint eraser to Jon, who caught it in midair.

[Isn't this a bit late?] Jon applied it to his fingertips and passed it to Rose, who used it on her fingertips.

"You're still going to touch door handles and such." I told

him.

"Point taken." Jon agreed.

Sloane was back. [Come on.]

I gave him my hand freely. I handed him the tube with my free hand. His right eyebrow went up and relaxed. He slid it into his pocket.

We darted down three different hallways. Finally, we found the restricted area. Unfortunately, the door was locked. Sloane slid the pin in front of the reader.

[I borrowed it from one of the guards.] Sloane told me.

The key panel changed colors and beeped softly. Sloane exhaled and pushed the door open. I grinned. I walked right into someone a foot taller than me. I looked up slowly to see angry eyes. Sloane had disappeared.

My Com translated his words automatically. "Who are you?"

I shrugged. The being reached for me. I took a step back. The being fell to the floor with a loud thud.

[Jahni, get behind me.] Sloane took my hand and pulled me towards him.

I heard a spray can. The being's expression settled into a peace and his eyes fluttered shut. Sloane let me go. I heard Sloane's footsteps.

[Where are you?] I asked.

"This way." Sloane said.

I followed his voice. Words were written on several doors. I didn't understand any of them.

Sloane opened another door. It was filled with several machines. Sloane appeared, and I shut the door behind us. He sat down at the Com in the middle.

I pulled up a seat beside him. "The footage of us entering the building needs to be deleted."

"You get that." Sloane delegated. "I'll get Jon's prints out of their system."

I was sitting in front of a different Com. I used it to access the security. As soon as I was inside of the system, I went to work deleting any evidence of Rose and I entering the building. I proceeded to delete the footage of Jon's detainment session. I searched further back and deleted Jon entering the building.

"Finished deleting Jon's prints from the system." Sloane

196

said.

"Good." I responded.

"I saw what could be a hidden camera." Sloane stood up and walked towards the only other door in the room besides the one we came through. "I think there is a separate feed in this room."

"Seriously?" I complained.

"Let me check." Sloane got up and came back. "There is."

Sloane deleted the footage of us in the control room. "We need to freeze the camera in the detainment room and here." Sloane searched the system and hit his fist on the table. "We don't have time for this."

"No, we don't." I leaned over his Com. "Here it is." I opened a separate screen and turned off the recording in both rooms.

"Thanks." Sloane's lips were a flat line.

"Let's make a break for it." I opened the door to leave and froze in place.

"What is it?" Sloane asked and followed my gaze to the

Com screen.

# 27

(Jon)

The door flung open.  I stood up in surprise.  Rose let out a scream.  She covered her mouth immediately.  I stood up in a movement and got in front of Rose.  Two rough looking guys stared at me.

"Come on!  We are busting you out of here."  One of them said.

I recognized the Fanith dialect immediately.  Ratillians trade with them often enough to make it a requirement for every Ratillian student to learn.  Growing up on Ratilles has some advantages.

"You don't even know me."  I replied.

"Don't have to."  One said.

"You can take your girlfriend too."  The other added.

They took each of us by the arm and pulled us out into the hallway, using each of us as a shield in case they were shot at. We were approaching the exit in record time. I couldn't think of a way to get out of their grasp without Rose getting hurt.

# 28

(Jahni)

My eyes were glued to the screen. The beings were headed down Jon and Rose's hall. I saw a large being pulling Jon and Rose out of the room.

[Sloane, we have got to get there now.] I told my husband.

[Done.] He took my hand in his.

We were invisible. As soon as he saw the hall, we were at the end of it. He looked through the door window and we were on the other side. We repeated this process five times. Each second that ticked away, the farther Jon and Rose were getting.

[We're not going to reach them in time.] I wanted to scream.

[If I didn't have to worry about walking through walls, we would have been there by now.] Sloane complained.

[I know.  We are not coming back to this planet ever again.]  I declared.

[Not even for refueling the Vaktow.]  Sloane agreed.

# 29

(Jon)

"Warning…Warning….Warning….Gyleer has escaped."
Blasted through every hall and every room.

[They are taking us outside Jahni.] I tried to let my
thoughts become an open book, so Jahni and Joe would know
what was happening.

They ushered us over to their ship. It was a FF300. You
only had one of those if you were going to do battle. It was the
stealthiest ship in this galaxy.

[Great.] I thought to anyone who would listen.

[They actually seem kind of nice.] Rose thought to me.

[Sure they are.] I let the sarcastic thought fly.

[Well, they did break us out.] Rose thought.

[Rosssseee.] I complained.

[What?] Rose thought innocently.

[I already told you, I didn't need broke out. They had nothing to hold me on. They probably wouldn't have known I was a Zellian by my fingerprints. Now, they have me on the assisted escape of a murderous felon. Which do you think is worse?] I told her.

[Oh, that didn't occur to me.] Rose thought back.

I shook my head in frustration. The door closed tightly behind us. We were staring at a three eyed being. I put on my most nonchalant attitude. I took the time to take in my surroundings and who we were dealing with.

Gyleer's teeth had turned green long ago. He smiled at us and drool came out the side of his lips. Elation surrounded him like a growing dome.

[Are you seeing what I'm seeing?] Rose asked. [That is the grossest thing this side of the galaxy.]

[You missed the episode of how sewage drains on Zalnorel's Believe it or Not, didn't you?] I thought to her.

[Why would you watch that, Jon?] Rose thought to me.

[It was on.] I shrugged.

"You're welcome." Gyleer said.

I expected a growl, but his voice was normal. He waited for a response. Rose wasn't going to say anything.

"Uh…thank you." I forced out the words.

He grinned. Rose was about to gag. He kind of reminded me of the bad guy on my favorite Com game Cranes Armor.

"What did they have you in for?" He asked.

I shrugged. "Those guys can't tell their criminals from their citizens."

Gyleer laughed. "I like you."

[Oh great! You made friends with him.] Rose thought to me.

[Better than enemies.] I thought back.

"Thanks." I said. [At least he won't be killing us.] I thought to Rose.

[You hope.] Rose countered.

"Where are we headed?" I asked.

I felt like I was playing a game of chance. On one hand, he was as likely to throw us out the Shuttle Car door as he was to answer.  He seemed like a talker, so we might have some hope.

"I have a place on the other side of the planet."  Gyleer answered.

[Will Jahni look for us there?]  Rose thought to me.

[I don't know.]  I thought back.

"You speak Fanith, why stay here?"  Rose was surprised.

Gyleer laughed.  "My people know thirty languages by the age of ten.  Fanith is only one of many."

"That's impressive."  Rose paid him a compliment.

He grinned at her.  "We are an impressive group."

"By your dialect and complexion, I very much doubt you are from Fanith."  Gyleer looked at us as if he could see into our souls.

[Jon!]  Rose panicked.

[Calm down Rose.  He knows nothing.]  I folded my arms.

Gyleer finally turned around.  He began joking with his comrades.  I breathed a slight breath of relief.

[We have to get out of here, Jon.]  Rose was scanning for a possible exit.

[Not now Rose, we have to wait for them to lose interest in us and then make a break for it.] It wasn't smart to leave now.

[If I see an out, we are taking it.] Rose told me.

[Okay.] I agreed.

Rose smiled. Gyleer didn't notice anything out of the ordinary. I tried to look over their shoulders toward the Com Screen, so I would have a general idea of where they took us in case we had the opportunity to backtrack. Gyleer moved in the way unintentionally and blocked my view.

[Rose, check the time on your Com.] It would be easier to get back if we knew how long it took to get there.

[Okay.] Rose tapped her Com on. [4:00]

[They aren't paying attention. Can you get a message to Jahni and Joe?] I asked.

[I think so.] Rose looked around. She tapped a few keys. [No signal.]

I fought the urge to scream. [Don't let them see it.]

She tapped the sides, and it went into stealth mode and blended in with her skin. Now it was a waiting game. Hopefully, we could get a signal in Gyleer's hideout.

[Jon, how long do you think we will be in here?] Rose asked.

[I don't know. An hour?] I guessed.

[What if we don't make it back home in a few days?] Rose asked.

[It won't be good for Zelle, I guess.] I answered her.

[What if we die?] Rose asked.

[Rose, we are not going to die.] I was getting frustrated.

[But we could die.] Rose told me.

[Do you really think God is going to let us die here with all we have been through?] I threw at her.

[I guess not.] Rose crossed her arms.

[He's not.] I told her.

She let out a heavy breath. [Sorry.]

[Me too.] I looked in the other direction.

*We're not going to die here, are we God?* I asked.

*No.* I felt God's reassuring answer.

The Shuttle Car landed. Gyleer stood up and led the way

of the ship.  Two of them trailed Rose and me.  They didn't trust us.  The Triz they were giving off said as much.  I did my best to act as if I didn't care.  They weren't buying it.

"Dwen, get the door."  Gyleer ordered.

The roof was coming off the building in front of us.  The windows had holes in them that looked like someone had used it for target practice.  Dwen opened the door.

"Nice place."  I commented about the disaster.

"It's home."  Gyleer grinned.

Rose was ready to vomit.  She held it in.  We were pushed through the door.  Gyleer walked over to a large chair and pushed a bunch of trash onto the floor.  He sat down and threw his legs up on the table.  A green grin covered his lips.

"Take a load off."  He ordered.

I brushed off some trash off the couch and a bug crawled away.  Great, now we are going to be infested.  I sat down.

[Jon, I can't sit there!]  Rose's thought was a roar.

[You better.]  I thought to her.  [Do you really want to get on Gyleer's bad side?]

[No.] Rose glared at me.

[Sit.] I ordered.

[Fine.] Her teeth were clenched as she barely sat on the seat. [I will have to burn this outfit, I hope you know.]

[K.] I agreed to end the conversation.

"Veebal, find us some food." Gyleer ordered.

Veebal got up obediently and left the room. He had a scar below his nose that ran across his mouth to his chin. His eyes were bloodshot. He answered in grunts when the others called him by name. Dwen was by his side most of the time. He talked enough for both of them.

Listening and watching would give us information. Unfortunately, Gyleer wanted us to talk. I wished they would put us in a room and forget us.

[I could always kick a hole through the roof and climb out. It didn't look like it would be too tough.] I suggested.

[Don't you dare!] Rose told me.

[Why not? All we have to do is wait until they leave us alone.] I told her.

[You're the one that said to play it safe.] Rose argued.

[Yeah, until we build some trust. I didn't want them to shoot us on the Shuttle Car. There are more chances to break out here.] I answered.

[Do you think Jahni and Joe will find us?] Rose thought desperately.

[We will get out of here and go home.] I promised.

[That's not what I asked.] Rose countered.

[It's what you meant.] I thought back.

[Yeah.] Rose agreed with a small smile of hope.

# 30

(Jahni)

[We have a missed message from Rose.] Sloane thought.

[I leaned forward to look at the Com. [When? Where are they? How long will it take to get to them?] I exploded.

[Twenty minutes ago. North about 40 kilometers, but they were on the move.] Sloane answered my questions.

I looked at the data Sloane was reading. The communication had only lasted for three seconds. [Not long enough for a message of any kind.] I let out a breath born of frustration.

[Maybe the message is that they are still alive.] Sloane thought.

[20 minutes ago they were, but are they now?] I asked.

"I don't know Jahni. I pray to God they are." Sloane said.

God. I closed my eyes tight. I needed God more right now than I have in a long time.

*Please God, watch over Jon and Rose. I love them so much. They are our responsibility. Dad put his trust in me and I failed him. The people of Zelle put their faith in me and I failed them too. You can protect them when I can't. Please help us find them alive. Keep them safe. In your holy name, amen.*

"Amen." Sloane echoed the last word of my prayer.

We got inside of the Vaktow and made our way to Jon and Rose's last known location.

# 31

(Jahni)

[Rose!] I thought loudly. I listened carefully for a response.

Sloane took my hand and squeezed it for support. [We will find them.]

[Yes, but you've heard what kind of being Gyleer is. What will he do to Rose?] I was getting hysterical.

[Jon is with her. He would die before he would let anything happen to her.] Sloane's thought was soothing.

The problem was my overactive imagination. Suddenly, a vision of Gyleer and two thugs from the Com took over my thoughts. They were going after Jon, who jumped out of the way of the two thugs. Jon spun around and elbowed Gyleer in the stomach. Gyleer groaned and stood up in a roar. He projected his arm into Jon's chest, Jon and went flying, and hit his head on the edge of the table. Jon slumped to the floor and didn't move. The two thugs stood over Jon's body, laughing.

"Jahni." Sloane whispered. "They can both handle themselves better than that."

"Are you sure?" Tears welled up in my eyes.

"Yes." Sloane answered.

I caved into his chest. "Why can't we find them?"

"It's only been two days. We have two more before it starts to effect Zelle." Sloane added.

"That's not why I'm worried." I whispered against his chest.

"I know." He stroked my hair downward in a soothing motion.

"If they could contact us, they would." I said.

"Yes, unless Gyleer took their WCs." Sloane spoke calmly.

I looked up at Sloane and smiled. "In that case they are fine."

Sloane exhaled. "Probably."

"Should we ask for help?" I asked.

Sloane was thoughtful. "Adeam might be able to assist us."

I bit my lower lip. [He would contact Dad. I don't want Dad to worry.] I paused. [We need the help. Use the Com.]

Sloane used the Com to contact Adeam. Uncle Adeam was on the other side of the Com within seconds. His brow furrowed. He read our Triz carefully.

"I don't see Jon or Rose, and you're worried." Uncle Adeam said.

"They were broke out of prison." I told him.

His eyes widened. "Why were they in prison?"

"They weren't." Sloane said.

"Maybe I should start from the beginning." I told my uncle.

"I think that might be best." Uncle Adeam looked over his shoulder. "Reroute to their destination."

"Yes, sir." Someone answered on Uncle Adeam's ship.

# 32

(Jon)

"What is that?" Dwen took my WC out of my hands.

I had hid it in my sock when I was being transported to the prison. I thought they might feel it on my wrist and take it.

Dwen looked at my WC frontward and backward. He threw it on the floor and stepped on it. The WC was unscathed. He stomped on it again. It was fine.

"What is this made of?" Dwen glared at me.

It wasn't my fault. I wasn't making him fail. He was doing that all by himself. It was kind of funny, but I wasn't about to show it.

I shrugged. "It tells time."

[Jon!] Rose accused.

[Hey, I'm telling the truth.] I told her.

[That's not all it does.] Rose thought to me.

[What should I do Rose? Tell him it's our way out of the shack?] I asked.

217

[No.]  She sulked.

[Should I tell him it can go underwater, survive extreme heat, and send off a distress signal?]  I let the sarcasm saturate my thoughts.

[No, you can't say that.]  Rose told me.

[But it does have a clock.]  I threw back at her.

[It does.]  She agreed begrudgingly.

[You could tell him about the design your own clothing feature.]  Rose suggested.

[Really Rose?  You honestly want me to tell a guy who barely bathes how to dress pretty?]  I didn't know where she got half of her ideas.

[I guess not.]  She agreed as she studied him.

Dwen went to the closet in the corner of the room and came out with a large hammer.  He swung it back, and it landed on the WC with a loud thud.  One of the roof tiles fell from the ceiling.  Dwen reached down and picked up the pristine Wrist Com.

Dwen put it down on the floor and hit it with the hammer eight more times.  The shelf on the back wall fell in a crash to the ground.  He wiped the sweat from his brow and bent down and grabbed the WC again.  It looked as if it was taken out of the box a few seconds ago.

[We need to write Com Com about that.]  Rose thought.

[Yeah.] I agreed, thoroughly impressed.

Dwen took the laser Model 231 out of his holster and aimed it at the WC. A shield surrounded the WC and absorbed the heat, turning it into extra battery life for the WC later. I waited to see if he would shoot it again. It was impressive to watch, but he stood there in stunned silence.

Finally, he gave up and put the Wrist Com on his wrist. He glared at us both. We watched him with a blank stare. The laser he had shot the WC with could easily be used on us if he were angry enough.

[Why isn't that in the commercial?] I frowned.

[It should be.] Rose agreed.

[We could advertise for Com Com.] I threw out the idea.

[Hmm. I can see it now; Princess and Prince of Zalnorel endorse Com Com's WC. You should too. Stores open every day with the exception of major holidays.] Rose nodded her agreement.

[Good tagline, we should use that in business class.] I laid dibs on the idea first. I was actually [looking forward to that class when we went back.]

[I'm not.] Rose thought. [I don't like adding up the numbers.]

[You're great at it.] I told her in confusion.

[I am, but I don't like it.] Rose was indignant.

[Same reason you don't do your mail?] I asked.

[I do my mail.] Rose protested.

[Only because I throw it on your bed.] I told her.

[Jon, you need to let that go.] She was getting irritated.

[Sure. I'll drop it, but next time I get my mail, I am still going to pour yours on your bed.] I let her have the truth.

[Probably a good idea, even though I don't want to admit it.] Rose conceded.

[You really should check out your office sometime.] I told her.

[Why bother?] She asked.

[Jalen puts your fan flowers in there.] I replied.

[I get flowers?] Rose was shocked.

[Yeah, I do too.] I admitted.

[You're kidding?] Rose didn't believe me.

[Not at all.] I replied.

[What do you do with them?] Rose asked.

[Leave them in my office most of the time. I gave them to Jalen once and a few times I sent them home with Salaranda. What do I need flowers for?] I let out a deep breath.

[You should have told me.] Rose declared.

[Even I know you'd be mad if I poured them on your bed, but if you want me to…] I offered.

[No!] Rose was horrified.

# 33

(Jon)

The floorboard creaked. My eyes shot open. I didn't move. I was looking at the tips of worn-out boots about six inches from my nose.

"What are we going to do with them?" I recognized the being in the boots as Veebal.

"Nothing for now." Gyleer said.

"We can't trust them." Veebal said.

"Possibly." Gyleer was thoughtful.

"Gyleer." Veebal said.

"Vee, you go too far." Gyleer said.

"Sorry." Veebal answered.

"I will sleep now. Leave them until I decide if you are

221

right." Gyleer said.

"Yes, sir." Veebal agreed.

They both left the room. I let out a deep breath. I listened to their thoughts; they had no plans to return any time soon. That left me and Rose in here alone for a while.

[Rose wake-up.] I thought to her.

Why did she have to take so long to wake up? I sat up and crawled on my knees the few feet it would take to reach her. The floorboard creaked under my weight. I held my breath and didn't budge.

I listened. No one heard a sound. Good. I gently lifted Rose's arm towards me and slid off her Wrist Com. As soon as I had it in my hand, she pulled her arm under her head. I turned it on. It actually got a signal this time.

It was too risky to talk. I activated the keyboard. Lights shot out to reveal the letters on the hard floor. I looked around. The room was still empty. I quickly typed.

*Get here already!* I inserted the coordinates on the Com and sent it to Jahni and Joe's Com.

I slid the Com on my wrist. I heard movement. I hit the

stealth button and hit the floor in a hurry.

"Good, they are still asleep." Dwen walked out of the room again.

I sat up. Rose's eyes fluttered open. She didn't move.

[You going to lie there all day?] I asked.

[I think something is crawling on my leg.] Rose thought back.

I got up and checked her leg. A bug the size of my thumb was crawling toward her knee. Ut oh. She wouldn't like that. I flicked the bug on the floor and stepped on it with my shoe.

[Thanks Jon.] Rose shivered.

[No problem.] I answered.

[At least they left us alone.] Rose said.

[Yeah. I sent a message to Jahni and Joe.] I told her.

Rose sat up. [What did they say?]

[They didn't get back.] I answered.

Rose felt her wrist. [What happened to my WC?]

[How do you think I got the message out?] I thought

back.

[But you lost yours!] Rose complained.

[It's not my fault that Dwen took it.] I told her.

[I want mine back.] Rose held out her hand.

[Whatever.] I slid it off and tossed it at her.

Rose caught it and slid it on her wrist. She smiled. I climbed onto the couch.

[They will come. They always do.] I thought to Rose.

She looped her arm through mine and leaned on my shoulder. [I know they do.]

[Good, stop acting like it's the end of our world.] I grinned.

[I will try. I guess.] Rose smiled back.

# 34

(Jahni)

"They sent us a message!" I grabbed Sloane's waist in excitement.

"It has their coordinates." Sloane checked his wrist.

"Let's go." I practically drug Sloane towards the Vaktow. We have been scouring every town we came to. This was the first glimmer of hope in days.

[There is an easier way.] Sloane chuckled and popped us inside of the Vaktow.

Sloane popped into his seat and inserted the coordinates that Jon sent. I plunged into my seat and buckled up. The Vaktow went upwards.

"What?" Something was off about Sloane's Triz.

"It'll take two hours to get there." Sloane responded.

"Is that all?" I asked.

"It's in a rocky area. The terrain is perfect for hiding a small shack. It might be hard to locate, even with the correct coordinates."

I groaned. "God will help us." I told him fervently.

Sloane smiled. "Sure will."

"Can you go faster?" I leaned back in my seat.

The Vaktow picked up speed. I hated waiting. My anxiety was on edge, but my war face was on point.

"Smeltzer, it's better if you go in on foot first." Uncle Adeam told my husband.

Sloane nodded.

"They won't be able to see you coming." Uncle Adeam smiled.

"I'm going with him." I was not about to let them bench

me.

"I figured you would, Jahni." Uncle Adeam nodded his approval. "He is one of the fiercest creatures on that planet."

"I know." I commented.

"Be careful." Uncle Adeam ordered.

"I will." I agreed.

"That means, don't take any chances." Uncle Adeam knew me too well.

[No more than necessary.] I thought to Sloane so Uncle Adeam could not overhear.

"She will be safe." Sloane answered for me.

[Thanks Babe.] I slid my fingers into his hand.

[Any time.] Sloane gave my hand a squeeze.

"Don't worry about me. You will be there for backup." I made an attempt to reassure my uncle.

Sloane looked at me sideways. His Triz questioned if I doubted his abilities.

[Okay, we can do it without his help.] I smiled.

[That's better.] Sloane grinned.

Uncle Adeam's brows furrowed together. "I know, but you are going in before we arrive. I wanted to make sure you take certain precautions."

"We will." Sloane told him.

"That's all I ask." Uncle Adeam's face smoothed over.

"I love you." I told Uncle Adeam.

His face softened. "I love you too."

"Until next time." I finished.

"Until next time." Sloane echoed.

"Until next time." Uncle Adeam was still observing us intently when I cut off communication.

# 35

(Jon)

[Jon, we are running out of time.] Rose's thoughts were getting desperate.

She had a point. I didn't want to just bail. Let's face it, if someone was going to shoot you in the back as you tried to run, it would be Gyleer or Veebal. Even Dwen. We had eighteen hours to get back to Zelle before the planet started to die. We had to get back. What was Dad thinking, letting us leave? I wanted to be angry with someone.

[Dad told Jahni, he wasn't going to make us stay on Zelle. He didn't think it was right.] Rose told me.

[Fine, whatever.] I leaned against the wall.

What were the chances they would all fall asleep at once? I looked around. Two of them were crashing on the floor and three others were outside having target practice. Not good chances. I thought Jahni and Joe would have been here by now.

[If someone could wake up easier, we could probably make a break for it at daybreak.] I thought to Rose.

[Jon, you know I can't help it.] Rose complained. [Besides, that would be too late.]

[Yeah, I know.] I thought back. [And I guess I can't leave without you.]

[You wouldn't do that.] Rose glared at me.

[You're sure?] I asked.

I wouldn't. She knows I wouldn't, but it sure would be easier. I could have escaped yesterday and the day before.

[What are you going to tell Dad when you make it home without me?] Rose crossed her arms.

[Depends if I'm the youngest, it might work out.] I grinned.

"Jon!" Rose exclaimed.

The being closest to us swatted his nose. I laughed. Rose put her hand over her mouth.

[See what you did.] I thought.

230

[Jon Julian! I didn't do anything.] Rose's thoughts boomed back.

[Whatever sister dear.] I smirked.

[This is not helping us with an escape plan.] Rose changed the subject.

[Okay genius, what kind of plan do you have?] I asked.

[I don't have one.] Rose admitted.

I nodded. "Hmm."

I stood up. No one noticed Rose's outburst. Our 'guards' slept through it.

"Jon." Rose hissed.

"Calm down Rose." I told her.

I paced the room. I heard shots being fired outside, so I walked over to the window. Gyleer was shooting targets out of a tree. I wanted to give it a shot.

[Jon, you seriously need to sit down.] Rose demanded.

[You seriously need to calm down.] I told her.

She put on a pout. I turned around and stared at her. She was really bad about pouting. She just didn't have any skill.

[Rose, that's terrible.] I referred to her pout.

[I've been working on it, isn't it getting any better?] She asked.

"No." I shook my head.

Rose scrunched up her face in disappointment. [I guess I better keep trying.]

[I'm sure I can do it better.] I thought smugly.

"I don't believe you." Rose was indignant.

"Believe me." I told her.

She stared me down. [I want to see.]

[Fine.] I took several strides across the room until I was within a few feet. I put on my pouty face.

"Wow! That was good." Rose admitted. [You really shouldn't be better at that.]

I shrugged. "If you have the gift, you have the gift."

Rose's nose twitched as she tried again. [Was that it?]

I shook my head no. [Rose you should give it up.]

Rose sighed. [For now.]

# 36

(Jahni)

[Jon!  Rose!]  I thought as loudly as I could manage.

[Jahni!]  Rose's thought hit me in a wave of desperation and happiness.

[Can you see us?]  Jon asked.

[No, we can't.]  Sloane replied.  [There is a building not too far from here.  Two guys are outside shooting a tree.]

[That's us!]  Rose exclaimed.

[Three of them are in here with us.]  Jon filled us in.

[Thanks Jon.]  Sloane was sincere.  [Jahni?]  Sloane held out his hand.

I took it eagerly.

[They're not paying attention.]  Sloane pointed out.

They aimed at the target and put their finger on the trigger. A loud explosion went off.

"Whoa."  One of them let off a cheer.

"Good shooting."  The target had a big hole in it.

[Sloane.] I thought in concern.

"You can do better than that!" One patted him on the back.

"I'll try it." He took a few paces backwards.

[Come on.] Sloane tugged at my hand.

Apprehension befell me as I followed his lead. I glanced down. The little bit of grass we encountered shrank beneath our weight and crumbled apart. My teeth were clenched. My body was on high alert. After what seemed like ages, Sloane popped us in front of the shack. We were in front of the window. I peered in. Sloane kept a tight grip on my fingertips.

[I am not making the same mistake I did when we were on Ratilles.] Sloane informed me.

[Sorry, I didn't realize I was about to pull out of your grasp.] I held his fingers just as tight.

[I know.] He told me.

The door flew open squeaking and hit the side of the shack with a thud, followed by more squeaking and another thud as it hit the shack again.

The one who opened the door, kicked it in disgust. Dust flew up from the ground and fell from the ancient roof. He wiped the dust from his eyes. He walked off the porch and headed to the guy's shooting.

[One down.] Sloane thought.

[Two to go.] Jon told us.

Sloane pulled me through the wall. The floor board squeaked. I grimaced.

"What was that?" Someone asked from the other room.

"Go check on it, Dwen." The other one growled.

The clumpy steps headed our way. Dwen stopped about six inches from Sloane's face. Sloane closed his mouth tight, so Dwen would not feel his breath. I was tucked behind Sloane, looking out.

"I don't see nothin'!" Dwen turned around and headed back.

[Are you in the same room with them?] I asked Jon and Rose.

[No.] Jon answered first.

[We are in the room past them.] Rose added.

I groaned. Footsteps came across the room again. This time it was not Dwen.

"I know I heard something." He grumbled.

Sloane pulled me back outside. [I think we can get them out this way.]

Sloane and I walked several feet and walked through the wall again. Jon and Rose stood up, waiting. I pulled away from Sloane and ran to give them both hugs. They threw their arms around me.

[Let's get out of here.] Sloane told us.

[Uncle Adeam is on his way to clean up these guys.] I told Jon and Rose.

[Good.] Rose responded.

[He has my WC and I want it back. Dad gave it to me.] Jon crossed his arms.

[Seriously?] Sloane asked.

[If you could.] Jon let his arms drop.

[I can.] Sloane was gone before I could beg him not to go.

In a flash, he was back, holding Jon's WC. Jon grinned from ear to ear. He took it from Sloane and slid it on his wrist.

[Thanks bro.] Jon told Sloane.

[Yeah, yeah…now can we go?] Sloane asked.

[Duh.] Rose responded.

We each latched onto Sloane's arm and walked through the wall. A few blinks later and we were standing by the Vaktow. Sloane walked us through the wall. We each took our seats. Sloane started it and was in the air as soon as the last belt was buckled. We were thrown back into our seats. I was never so glad to leave a place as I was at that moment.

I turned on the Com and connected the line with my father. Dad answered immediately. Uncle Adeam was standing next to him. Dad peered through the screen until he saw Jon and Rose in the backseat. He was relieved.

"We have them!" I told my father on the Com.

"Thank God!" Dad exclaimed.

"How did you get to Uncle Adeam so quickly?" I asked.

"New Vaktow of yours arrived yesterday. I knew you wouldn't mind if I borrowed it." Dad answered.

"So it is faster." I looked at Sloane.

Sloane had a brief moment of elation before his jaw tightened. "Jahni, we have a problem."

That was never a good sign. I scanned the monitors. That's when I saw it. We were being followed. Their ship was faster than ours.

"We're not going to make it." Sloane told me.

"What's going on?" Dad demanded.

"We are being followed." Sloane told him.

"Take cover." Dad told us solemnly. "We are on our way."

"Okay." Sloane responded by making the Vaktow dive down.

Dad faded off the Com Screen. I looked nervously back at my siblings. Jon looked determined, and Rose appeared startled. Both of their Triz revealed they were concerned.

Sloane scanned the other ship. "This is getting worse."

"What is?" I asked.

"They have weapons that will destroy the Vaktow with

one hit and they have more than thirty defensive weapons onboard that scans are picking up." Sloane concentrated on his driving.

"What about shields?" Rose asked.

"Stealth mode?" Jon added.

Sloane shook his head no. "Stealth mode can't block their scans. Our shields are inferior to theirs."

"Define inferior?" I said it like a question.

"One bomb and we say hello to God with our shields at full-strength." Sloane grimaced.

"I want to see God, but not today." Rose said.

"What do we do?" Jon asked.

The three of us looked at Sloane expectantly. His jaw tightened. That was never a good sign. We were in big trouble.

"Out run them." Sloane answered.

"You said our ship is inferior." Jon responded.

I didn't like where Sloane's thoughts were going. I knew before Sloane's words came out. We were going to literally be running. The Vaktow took a dive. Sloane unbuckled. The Vaktow was on thought command. I gulped and unbuckled as well. Rose was petrified, but did the same. Jon was standing up before Rose. He grabbed his bag out of the back seat and slung it over his shoulder.

I slid my fingers into Sloane's hand. Rose and Jon

touched his forearm, and we disappeared.

# 37

The enemy ship landed. Several guys had hit the ground running. Sloane popped us several yards away. We bolted through the shrubbery. It would only be a matter of time before Dad and Uncle Adeam found us.

I fought to keep up Sloane's brisk pace as we eluded the beings threatening our lives. Lasers fired, I ducked. Sloane slowed down enough to make sure we were all safe. He pushed me under a limb and the ground beneath us crumbled. We slid several yards underground. The thoughts of the beings were getting louder. It was only a matter of time before they discovered us.

"Where are we?" Rose asked.

"How am I supposed to know?" Jon retorted.

Sloane placed a finger to his lips. [They can hear you.]

[Sorry Joe.] Rose thought.

We were underground. I placed my hand against the side

of the wall.  It was hard and concrete.  We were in a cave.  The only light came from the hole we fell through.  Jon pulled his backpack off his shoulder, unzipped his bag, and turned on a flashlight.  Rocks fell from above us.  We heard murmuring and more rocks fell.  They would be after us in seconds.

[Let's get out of here.]  Sloane pulled my hand away from the hole.

The way behind us had caved in.  We hurried in the other direction, praying for an escape.  Sloane could walk through the walls, but we were underground.  Popping up and over was not his strong point.  Some things got stuck when he did that.  Personally, being part of a piece of granite is not how I want to die.

The cave narrowed.  We had to walk single file.  It wasn't long before we were walking sideways to get through.  It didn't appear to narrow any further.

"I know I asked for an adventure, but this is ridiculous."  Jon blew off steam.

"Be careful what you ask for."  Sloane commented.

"Ha ha, very funny."  Jon blew him off.

"No, I mean it.  You might get it."  Sloane reiterated.

I felt a hand land on my head.  I took my right hand and grabbed his wrist in an iron grip.  I ducked under his arm, taking his wrist with me.  He slunk downward when I used my body weight to get the upper hand.  Before he could retaliate, I took my fist to his face.  I let go of his wrist and I heard him groan as he hit the floor.

"That was too close."  Sloane grabbed my hand and pulled me by his side.

Jon scanned the light behind us.  No one was in sight.  We listened for thoughts, but didn't hear any besides the groaning one on the floor.  We hurried to make our escape.  The light from Jon's flashlight was barely lighting our path as we made haste along the small walkway.

Finally, the cave widened.  We kept listening for thoughts beside our own, but didn't hear any.  The only sound around, came from us.

"Dad should be here by now."  Rose said.

"I don't know how far away he was.  I wasn't paying attention."  I admitted.

"Joe?"  Jon asked.

Sloane closed his eyes and focused on what he had seen.  A hologram formed around us.  We were inside of the Vaktow.  The Screen popped up.  Sloane's eyes popped open.  He scanned the screen.

"We have ten or fifteen minutes before they reach us.  We gotta find a way out of here."  Sloane told us.

"If we walk through that wall…"  Jon began.

"If we walk through that wall, there is a good chance I might lose all of you." Sloane was looking at me like I was the most precious thing in four galaxies.

"Well, let's try something different. How about you walk through the wall and come back?" Jon suggested.

Sloane thought over the plan carefully. "That might work."

Sloane disappeared through the wall. Jon held up his flashlight, so we could see his return. It was almost a minute before he walked back to us.

"There is no way." Sloane shook his head no. "I can't guarantee your safety. It's too far."

Jon let his hand fall that contained the flashlight. "Okay, there has to be a way out of here."

"Someone built these tunnels." I told them. "All we have to do is follow them. Hopefully, our Wrist Com's are detectable through this." I pointed at the ceiling.

Sloane got a funny look across his face. I knew that look like the back of my hand. I didn't need to hear Sloane's thoughts to know what it meant, but I asked anyway.

"They're not detectable in here, are they?" My hope dimmed.

Sloane shook his head no again. "I'm sorry."

"Dad, will find us. He has to find us." Rose responded.

"Correction, we'll find him." Jon told her.

"Then we'll find him, and that's all there is to it." Rose marched down the tunnel.

All four of our Wrist Com's went off.

"It's Dad!" Rose yelled excitedly.

Rocks crumbled from the side of the cave walls, because of the echoes.

"Rose, don't yell." Jon ordered my sister.

"Where are you at?" I asked.

"We found the other ship." Dad responded. "We have it surrounded. When they come back, they won't have a chance."

"Good." Jon said.

"Exactly." Dad agreed. "Now where are you guys at? I don't see your location on the monitor."

"I'm surprised you're getting through at all." I said.

"We fell down a hole and were inside an underground cave." Jon explained.

"Let's see if we can get out of here a little bit faster." Sloane urged us to hurry up.

We heard the rush of water. When we came around the bend, we came to a halt. Water was flowing into the cave in a rushing waterfall.  Jon illuminated the area with his flashlight.  I looked down.  The water was only a few yards away from the ledge.

"How did a waterfall get down here?"  Rose asked.

I shrugged and looked at Sloane.  He was examining the depths and speed of the water.  He looked for an escape, but didn't see an exit.

"Must be a river of some kind.  Either from the top or the bottom.  It's not coming up, so it must be going out." Jon said.

"There has to be a way out."  Sloane agreed.  "The question is, how do we find it."

Rose looked over the ledge uncertainly.  There was no way out, but the direction we had come and the water before us.  Both options were bad.

"I'll go."  Jon offered.

"Not without me."  Sloane crossed his arms.

I bit my bottom lip.  [I don't like this.]

Sloane pulled my chin up to meet his gaze.  "I love you."

[I know.]  I replied.

[That's not the right answer.]  His grin said that he won.

[I love you too.]  I added.

[Good.]  Sloane leaned in for a kiss.  [I'll keep him safe.]

[I know.]  I answered.  "We need to pray."

Sloane nodded his agreement.  Jon set his legs a shoulder

width apart and bowed his head. Rose held both of her hands tightly and closed her eyes.

"Dear God, please watch over Sloane and Jon. Keep them safe. We need to get out of here so we can get back home. Please protect us and help us find a way out of here safely. I need them. Don't let anything bad happen to them. In your name amen." I finished.

I really didn't want Jon to go, but I knew he wouldn't stay. That meant I had to stay behind with Rose. I looked down at the water. The current wasn't too strong.

# 38

(Jon)

I took the step over to the cliff. The water was rushing. Some of it came up and splashed the tips of my shoes. I've seen faster. The edge of the ledge was slightly damp, but not muddy. I didn't think I was in any danger of slipping and falling.

"So I guess you don't want me to pat you on the back." Joe chuckled.

I smirked. "Probably not the best idea. I am your back up."

Joe reached out his hand like he was going to give me a push.

"Sloane!" Jahni's voice went up an octave.

Joe laughed loudly. You could hear the echoes off the walls. Joe took off his shirt and handed it to Jahni. She hugged the shirt. Her worried Triz hit in seconds. Joe leaned forward and kissed her. She frowned.

"We will be fine." Joe reassured her.

"Be safe." Jahni separated each word and looked at both of us.

Those two words were full of emotions that I didn't want to dwell on.

"Yeah, yeah, whatever Jahni." I avoided answering.

"Good, you understand." Rose added hastily.

I laughed. It broke into an awkward exhale. My nerves were starting to get to me. I wasn't thrilled about the idea of jumping in, but it had to be done. I pulled my shirt off and dropped it onto my backpack.

I took a deep breath. [Ready.]

[Let's do it.] Mr. Fearless jumped in first.

I wasn't about to let him win. I exhaled again and took another breath before I dove off the cliff. I heard Joe make a splash and then I felt the water swallow me whole. The water was a little chilly. I was almost used to the cold when my head surfaced. Joe was there waiting for me.

"Looking good." Rose gave us a thumbs up.

Jahni was biting her bottom lip. Joe gave her a wave and a smile. Jahni gave a weak wave back. We both took another breath and dove downward.

I pointed my flashlight in front of me. A large beacon exploded from Joe's WC. It was easy to go down the first few feet. After that, I had to use the rocky wall to get myself further down.

[I see something.] Joe thought.

[Where?] I scanned the area.

Joe was right in front of me. I let go of the wall to get a closer look.

[I need air.] I thought to Joe.

[Okay, I'll get some too.] Joe turned around and headed to the surface with me.

[Could you have held your breath longer?] I was curious.

[About a minute or two more.] I could hear the smirk in his thoughts.

[Of course you could.] I drenched the thought in sarcasm.

[What did you think I did on Deltik? Just chill out for half of my life.] Joe was trying to make a point.

[What are you talking about?] I asked.

[Me and a few of the guys I went to school with used to practice holding our breath. I always won. I was up to about six minutes for a little while.] Joe told me.

[Seriously?] I asked.

[Yep.] He answered. [Unfortunately, I'm down to about five minutes now.]

[Show off.] I threw at him.

[Any time I can.] Joe quipped.

[Cut the chitchat.] Rose told us. I heard her giggling

when I came up for air.

"So, does it look like we can get out of here?" Jahni asked.

"We'll get out of here." Joe responded.

"I know that." Jahni sighed.

"Come on." Joe nodded towards me and went downward.

I was at his heels. We headed straight for the area that Joe had thought looked promising.

[Two minutes.] Joe's thought was full of mirth.

[Shut up.] I threw back. [We can't all be good at everything.]

[I know, but someone does come close.] Joe referred to himself.

[Humble too.] I teased.

I pushed forward to catch up with Joe. I was an arm's length behind him.

[I think it's flowing out that way.] Joe indicated with his WC.

[You might be right.] I agreed.

[We need to get down there.] Joe told me.

I kicked forward. The cave sloped into a tunnel. It was about three yards in diameter. I didn't mind tight spaces, but this was making me nervous. The water was much colder down here. Joe was above me when I looked upward. His eyes were looking straight ahead, focused on getting out of this tunnel.

[About ninety seconds of air left?] Joe asked.

[I think so.] I hoped so. I better start praying it is so.

We could see light at the end of the tunnel. At least I thought it was light.

[Point your flashlight behind you.] Joe hid his WC against his chest.

I moved the flashlight behind me. It was definitely brighter in front of us. I felt a huge relief come over me.

*[Thanks God.]* I prayed.

I pushed out half a breath of air to expel some of the carbon dioxide from my body. I was fairly confident I would be able to breathe fresh air soon.

Joe put his WC in front of him again. I pointed my flashlight forward. It was several arm's lengths before we arrived at the source of the new light. I was hoping it was the sun and not some other unknown light.

My head hit the surface. Joe was already looking at me. It was daylight that we saw, but we were still in the caves. Light was coming through the roof. The water took up most of the empty space. There was a rock shore a few yards across and a few yards wide.

"Where are we at?" I asked.

Joe shrugged. "Your guess is as good as mine."

"Can we at least get out of here?" I looked around, unsure.

"Let me see." He answered.

The rocky shore was a good foot above the water. Joe pulled himself up onto the ledge. I swam a few strokes toward the rocky ledge. I saw a path curving around a large boulder. It went somewhere.

"I don't like it." I referred to the path.

"We don't have to follow it." Joe told me.

Joe looked upward. Before I knew it, he was sitting on top of the opening. He grinned down at me.

"Show off." I laughed.

"Yep." Joe said proudly before standing up and looking around. "This looks promising."

"Should we go get the girls?" I secretly dreaded going through the tunnel again. I hated not having the opportunity to come up for breath.

"Can you make the swim back?" Joe asked.

"Of course." I scoffed. I was not about to let him go back without me and show me up.

Joe took off on a dive toward the water and disappeared. He reappeared about a foot above the water and did a perfect dive. He came up for air and ran his fingers through his hair.

"You really…that is a sweet trick." I wish I could do that.

"I know." Joe grinned.

We took a breath and headed the way we had come. It seemed to go much faster on the way back than it had before. Maybe that's because we knew where we were going. It wasn't long before our heads were resurfacing.

Rose was grinning. Jahni smiled. She was utterly relieved.

"You two are a bunch of sissies." I told them.

"Yeah, yours." Rose laughed at her own joke.

I laughed with her.

"Alright, I'm ready." I was done with using flashlights to light the way.

"What about your backpack?" Rose held it up.

I cringed. "Drop it."

"Whatever you say." Rose let it go.

"Can I get that in writing?" I caught my bag.

"Wouldn't do you any good. Everything in that bag is going to be soaked." Rose did a cannonball.

Water came up and hit my face. I brushed it off, but it wasn't like it did much good. I was about to dive under anyway.

I pulled the bag onto my back. "When we get back to Zelle, I'm going to need to remember to get a waterproof bag for the next trip."

[I think I'm done with these trips.] Jahni thought to us.

[Why?] Rose complained.

"Shut up Rose, we'll get her later." I winked.

"Okay. I really had a blast!" Rose exclaimed.

[We have the gangsters chasing us and you're having a blast?] Jahni thought she was crazy.

[Absolutely.] Rose responded. [Who else can say they were captured like three times, chased into a cave, and dove through underwater caverns on their break? No one! We totally nailed that report.]

[I have to go with her on this one.] I agreed. [Though, I doubt we have to write a report. It's only two weeks.]

[Still, they always ask us what we did.] Rose dove into the water with a grin on her face.

[Right.] I thought.

Jahni was the last one to jump in. She aimed carefully so she wouldn't run into any of us. Her head bobbed up closer to Joe's.

Joe kissed her on the forehead, then her lips. "See we're fine. No need to worry."

[Still working on that one.] Jahni responded.

Joe grinned. "Let's go for a swim."

We plunged into the water. We were close to the opening, so we came up for one last breath. We entered the underground tunnel and Rose grabbed onto my ankle.

I shook her hand off. [What do you think you are doing?]

[Trying to get a lift.] Rose's thought was an attempt to appear innocent.

[Not on me.] I thought in exasperation.

I swam faster to prevent her from grabbing my ankle again. It wasn't too long before my head poked above the surface. Joe was smiling at us. Jahni spit out a mouthful of water before she swam the few strokes to dry land. Joe gave her a hand and pulled her to her feet. Rose and I headed that way too.

"Whoo." Rose rubbed her eyes and let her feet dangle into the water.

I rolled onto the shore and let out a heavy breath. I didn't want to admit it to anyone, but those swims took it out of me. I thought about the much longer swim I had taken to the island. It had been difficult, but it had been full of air. Holding my breath that long was not something I was used to.

"Just think of it as practice for the Zanxtear Race." Joe grinned.

"I think I'm trained up." I let my head rest on my arms.

Joe chuckled. "I guess."

"Let's do the checklist." Rose held up her hand. "Swimming, check." Rose held up one finger. "Running, definitely check." She held out a second finger. "Test portion, check. We ended break with midterms." Rose held up a third finger and made a horrible face. I laughed. "Last, but not least… fix a Vaktow. We didn't do that during break, but you do that at home for fun, so you're totally ready for the next Zanxtear Race."

"Thanks for the vote of confidence." I grinned.

"Not a problem." Rose's voice was a happy melody.

"Sooooo…How are we getting out of here?" Jahni asked.

"Like this." Joe disappeared. He was sitting at the top of the cave in the hole in the roof.

"Oooo, that looks like fun." Rose clapped her hands together.

"That's because it is." Joe yelled down.

A shadow fell over the opening. Someone hit Joe on the head and he fell from the roof and landed with a thud. Jahni's breath caught in her throat and I heard her gasp. Laughter floated downward.

"Stay down there." The laughter continued.

I didn't recognize the voice. Nor could I see their face. The sun was in my way. Joe was starting to sink. I dove into the water and started pulling Joe to shore. Jahni had pulled Rose against the wall.

I heard the shot and then saw them in the water. How in the world was I going to outrun bullets? Joe needed to wake up now. I shook him and continued to pull him.

[Sloane! Sloane! Get up now!] Jahni demanded.

I saw Joe's head move. He mumbled, and another shot went off. Joe looked up, and the water vanished from around my body and was replaced by cold air. We were thirty feet above the opening of the cave. I gulped. I loved heights, but this was ridiculous.

The being looked up and saw us. I thought I saw a look of confusion cross his face, but he was too far away. The gun aimed upward in our general direction and the bright sun was gone. We were sitting on the shore looking up at the being that had been shooting at us. My stomach clenched. This whole life flashing before my eyes was getting ridiculous. Would it be too juvenile to say, Daddy come save us?

I gulped in another breath. [Do something!]

Joe shook his head to clear his thoughts. He searched for Jahni, who ran to him and threw her arms around him. Rose touched Joe's arm.

[There's only one way to do this.] Joe thought to us.

[Do it.] Jahni thought urgently.

I heard a shot go off, but we disappeared before I saw where it landed. We were high in the sky looking at the back of the maniac, wasn't he out of ammo yet? Rose lost her grip and started falling. The next second, we were on the ground just below the opening of the cave on the opposite side of the shooting maniac. Thank God he didn't have good aim. I looked up to see

Joe catching Rose and then felt the air disperse to allow for their mass.

Rose threw her arms around Joe. "Thank you!"

Gravel slid down the side of the hill. The being fired the gun again. This time, the gun was pointed straight at my head. I took in a deep breath. Time seemed to slow down to nothing. There was no avoiding the bullet. Joe was a full foot away, being squeezed by my sister. He wouldn't make it.

I waited for the bullet that never came. I heard the click of the gun being fired again and again. It was out of ammunition just in time.

*Thank you God.* My prayer was sincere.

*I still have a plan for you, Jon.* God promised me.

*I'm glad. Very very glad.* I answered with relief.

Joe detangled himself from Rose and disappeared until he was in front of the being, who was fumbling with his pockets, trying to pull out an extra clip to fill the gun. Joe gave him a push and let him think he was going to hit the water before he caught him in midair. I rushed to the cave opening and looked down.

Joe dropped him into the water about a foot in the air. A big splash echoed off the walls. Joe stood beside me, grinning.

"That was amazing." Rose put her arms around us both.

Joe turned around to see Jahni standing there with arms crossed. Joe sauntered over, grinning. Jahni's fierce look faded and even I could tell he was forgiven for almost being shot.

"I hate to be a…whatever, but where is Dad with the Shuttle Car?" Rose asked.

I ran my finger through the air and traced the way we had come.

"Let me see if I can find what direction we came from." Joe went straight to his WC and started pushing buttons.

"That way." I pointed in the direction of the Vaktow.

"He's right." Joe's WC was flashing.

I grinned. "I got a good sense of direction." I nodded my head.

"Looks kind of rocky." Rose scanned the area.

"Let's just get home." Jahni sighed.

"That's my girl." Joe grinned. "My way?" Joe's smile went to hopeful.

"No Sloane." Jahni sputtered.

"But…" Joe's sentence trailed off into laughter.

"What's your way? Is it fast?" Rose was curious.

"I think I have an idea about his way." I told them.

"Soooo?" Rose wanted to know.

"Pop right about there." Joe pointed in the air. "Then I would see the Vaktow and we could just…you get the picture."

"Ooo. We should at least do that once." Rose rubbed her hands together.

"Already have." Jahni grumbled.

"Ditto." I agreed.

"Fine, let's take the boring fast way." Rose stomped her right foot one time.

Four pops later, we were standing in eyesight of the Vaktow. It was hard to believe we had traveled this far underground in a few hours.

"Home sweet home." Rose cheered.

"Not exactly." I shook my head.

"Well, it has been for the past two weeks, kinda." She added.

"You are nuts sista." I told her.

"Yeah, but you're related to me." Her smile was contagious, and I found myself smiling.

"No need to use those kinds of words." Jahni grinned.

At that, I couldn't help laughing.

"Hey, I think I've been insulted." Rose complained.

"If you weren't sure, she didn't do it right." I winked at Jahni.

Rose tried to look mad, but failed. She ended up grinning from ear to ear. She nudged Joe to take our final jump, and we were standing beside the Vaktow.

# 39

(Jahni)

Dad came running toward us as soon as Sloane landed us beside of the ship. He grabbed Jon and Rose in a hug immediately. He held them so tight neither of them could move.

"Dad, I can't breathe." Jon said.

Only then did he loosen his grip. "I have been worried like crazy."

"It's okay, Dad." Rose said.

"You're not going to cry, are you?" Jon asked.

Dad messed up Jon's hair. "Maybe."

"We should get home, Dad." Jon told him.

"You think." Rose chimed in.

"Well, the planet is about to deteriorate, so yeah it might

be a good idea." Jon retorted.

I laughed. "Get on the Vaktow."

"You heard the lady." Sloane said. "Besides, Mr. Sarcastic probably has a point…today."

"Gee thanks….Sloane." Jon grinned wickedly.

"Shut up and get in." Sloane pushed Jon towards the Vaktow.

Jon laughed and managed to escape Dad's grasp to get in. Rose followed quickly behind Jon. Dad wasn't about to let them out of his sight. He walked at a slower pace and stopped in front of me.

"Thank you, Jahni." My father hugged me.

"I'm sorry I lost them." I said into his shoulder.

He pulled back. "It wasn't your fault."

"But you put your trust in me." I was not going to cry, I told myself.

"You still have my trust, sis." His eyes were so sincere. Dad's Triz confirmed his words to be the truth.

"You forgive me?" I asked.

"There was nothing to forgive." Dad was earnest.

Tears gathered in my eyes. I pursed my lips together to help me hold back the tears. I gulped.

"No tears." Dad leaned forward, looking into my eyes to make his point.

"Okay." I answered in a croaky voice.

"You two coming?" Rose bellowed.

"No, they are making a campfire. You going to have a s'more with them?" Jon asked her.

I laughed. "Sure Rose, what's one more?"

Jon laughed. "Yeah, see plenty of room for you."

"Shut-up Jon." Rose told him.

He laughed harder. We took our seats. Sloane closed the door and pulled the Vaktow into the air.

The Com blinked once and an image of Uncle Adeam came on the screen. Sloane answered.

"We have Gyleer in custody. We are returning him to the authorities on this planet. We should be returning to Zelle soon." Uncle Adeam said.

"He's one bad dude." Jon nodded his head.

"I don't want to know what he would have done to us if we stayed there much longer." Rose shuddered.

"You are safe now." Dad patted her head.

"Yes, you are." Uncle Adeam agreed with a small smile. "Until next time." He nodded.

"Until next time." The five of us responded together, and the screen went dark.

I was so ready to be home in my nice warm bed, without worrying over my brother and sister. [I was not planning a trip off world with them ever again. Too much stress was involved, not to mention the guilt of losing them.]

[We don't have to go that far away, Jahni.] Jon thought to me.

"A little trip wouldn't be that bad." Rose added.

Sloane laughed. "Good luck with that one Babe."

I was hanging off my seat to look at them. "Not on your life. And with our luck it would be your life."

Jon laughed. "Oh Jahni, don't overdramatize it."

"Are you serious?" My voice went up a few octaves. "It was only supposed to be a few pit stops, fun parks, and educational stuff and you two have the nerve to get captured."

"Well, next time we won't ask to be detained, or a jailbreak the same day we end up talking to the nice security people." Jon grinned.

Rose's eyelashes fluttered. "We'll be good next time."

"It's too soon guys." Dad's mouth was in a straight line.

"Fine Daddy." Rose sighed.

"Next break, we'll hit you up." Jon winked.

I turned around. "Not off planet."

Jon chuckled. "I think that gives us a little leeway."

[Make them stop.] I thought to Sloane.

[Not sure I can.] Sloane admitted. "Why don't you guys wait until the devastation of getting you back wears off?"

"Good one." Jon said.

Rose sulked. "I guess."

"So, did anyone miss us?" Jon asked.

"Only half of Zelle." Sloane said.

"Really?" Rose perked up.

"Really. Not to mention your old Dad." Dad told them.

Rose giggled. "We already know you missed us."

"But I obviously don't count." Dad stressed the words.

"Nope." Jon laughed. "At least for Rose. I still love ya Dad."

"Hey, that's not what I meant!" Rose protested.

"It never is." Jon quipped.

"I love you Daddy. I really do." Rose told our father.

"I know you do, sweetie." Dad put an arm around her.

Rose stuck her tongue out at Jon. Jon laughed harder. Rose put her tongue back in her mouth. Her mouth turned into a frown.

"Way to be grownup about it, sis." Jon grinned and relaxed in his seat.

Sloane landed in the front yard.  Several people were holding signs, welcoming us back.  We walked out of the Vaktow and the crowd went wild.

[Wow!]  Jon thought.

[This is for us?]  Rose asked.

[We told you half of Zelle missed you.]  Our father thought.

[Yeah, but I didn't expect…]  Jon stopped mid-thought.

[All this.]  Rose finished.

[This is nothing.  Wait until we get inside.]  Dad told them.

[There's more?]  Rose asked.

[Yes.]  Dad told her.

The crowd parted so we could make our way up to the steps.  The crowd erupted with cheers.  I was amazed at the turnout.  The last time there had been a crowd this big, we had returned with Dad last year.  Honestly, this crowd was bigger.

[That's because they knew Jon and Rose were coming back.]  Sloane thought to me.  [Most of Zelle was unsure if we would return the first time.]

[I am always amazed at the amount of people that show up for us.] I was in awe.

Dad held up his hand. The crowd slowly died down. Every face waited expectantly.

"Thank you for all of your prayers, letters, and coming out to support us." Dad said.

The crowd exploded in cheers. They started chanting. "Prince and Princess."

Dad held up his hand. The crowd was quiet again. Dad moved aside and motioned Jon and Rose to come closer to the balcony. They did.

[You are up.] Dad thought.

[Rose?] Jon asked.

[I can go first.] Rose agreed.

"Thank you! I have never felt so loved as I do at this moment. You are the best people I know and I am so glad you are here." Rose said.

The crowd clapped and cheered. They started chanting.

"Prince Jon.  Prince Jon."

Jon held up his hand the way our father had.  The crowd went silent.  I was amazed at how good he was at this.

"I am in awe.  You have all risen higher than any of my expectations.  Thank you for being you and showing your love to the fullest.  This is not a day I or my sister will soon forget.  I could not ask to be Prince of a better people than the ones that belong to Zalnorel and I am honored by each one on Zelle who has shown that same love.  Thank you."  Jon finished his monologue.

The crowd erupted even louder than before.  It took them quite some time to become silent.  Finally, when the crowd did quiet down, Dad took over.

"Thank you once again.  Each of the children has had an exciting few days.  It is time to take it easy.  I am so glad to have them back.  Thank you."  Dad finished.

The crowd erupted into cheers and claps.  They were all standing with lit faces of excitement.  I was always in awe to see so many people who cared about us in one spot.  We each took a bow or curtsy.  We waved a hand in the air.  The crowd went silent.

"Until next time." Sloane, I, Jon, Rose, and Dad all said together.

"Until next time." The crowd echoed.

We went into the house. The hall was lined with flowers and cards. Rose's breath caught when the door opened. Jon moved far enough in so we could close the door.

"These are for us?" Rose asked.

"Yes." Salaranda entered from one of the rooms. "Princess Rose and Prince Jon, we are so glad to have you back."

"We are glad to be back." Rose hugged her.

[Do I hear my grandchildren in there?] G-Lil thought.

"G-Lil!" Rose said.

"I thoroughly pray you are not going to make a habit of this?" G-Lil told us.

"A habit of what?" Rose asked.

"Getting caught." G-Lil shook her head. "You should talk to your Uncle Adeamkenrick. He might be able to give you kids some pointers."

"I don't usually have any problems getting in and out

when I need to."  I slid my hand into Sloane's.

"Stupid security."  Sloane grumbled.

"No walking through walls?"  G-Lil gasped.  "It's not fun to have to use a door like the rest of us."  G-Lil winked.

Sloane shook it off.  "I guess not."

I squeezed Sloane's hand to give him support.  I knew it was frustrating to him to have that limitation put on him.  He smiled at me weakly.

# 40

"Jahni, how am I ever going to write all of these thank you notes?" Rose groaned.

I laughed. "Have Jon do it."

Rose made a face. "He already said no. I tried."

"Aren't half of them his?" I asked.

"Yes, but some of them are addressed to me personally, and he told me I had to do my own mail." She grumbled.

"He's so mean." I tried to help her.

She giggled. "I know, right?"

"I am not mean." Jon walked into the room.

"Are too." Rose grinned.

"I have my own mail to respond to. I am not filling out

thank you notes to half of Zelle by myself. It's just not going to happen. What's the use of having a twin if she doesn't do half of the work?" Jon told me.

I laughed. "He has a point, Rose."

"Are you taking his side again?" Rose asked.

"I don't take sides." I protested.

"Actually, you do." Sloane walked in.

"Hey!" Jon and Rose complained.

"Sloane!" I exclaimed.

Sloane zeroed in on me. His eyes twinkled. I waited. He was too attractive to be too mad at, even if he was getting me in trouble with my brother and sister.

"My side." He leaned in for a kiss.

"You're trying to cause trouble?" I pulled back before he could kiss me.

"If I can help it." He didn't let me go. "Are you going to kiss me or what?"

I laughed and kissed him. Rose and Jon made puking noises. Sloane laughed.

"Did we clear the room?" Sloane asked.

"Nope, they're still here." I looked at my siblings.

"Worth a shot." Sloane grinned.

[You are bad.] I thought to him.

[Only sometimes, when I can't help it.] Sloane thought to me.

[Okay, so twenty-three hours a day?] I asked with a smile.

[Maybe.] He grinned at me.

Dad walked in. "Dinner is ready."

"Sweet!" Jon exclaimed, and bolted out the door.

Rose strolled out the door as if she had all the time in the world. Dad laughed. I started to head out and Dad stopped us.

"Yes?" I asked.

Dad handed me a vanilla folder. "It's a lot of graphs and lofty language, but it breaks down to we are still on schedule for your mother's rescue. I think you are right, Jahni. She is still alive."

*The Zelle Saga*

*Book 4: Drex*

[https://www.amazon.com/gp/product/B01AS4INB0/ref=dbs_a_de](https://www.amazon.com/gp/product/B01AS4INB0/ref=dbs_a_de)

[f_rwt_bibl_vppi_i6](f_rwt_bibl_vppi_i6)

# Check out my page on Facebook!

https://www.facebook.com/Heidi-Harris-510080442485714/?

ref=bookmarks

# Heidi Harris' books are on Amazon!

*https://www.amazon.com/Heidi-Harris/e/B01758LK4E?*

*ref=sr_ntt_srch_lnk_3&qid=1591557444&sr=1-3*

# Zelle Saga

Deltik

Zelle

Jareneiks

Drex